if HOME *is a* PLACE

K. Linda Kivi

POLESTAR
BOOK PUBLISHERS

IF HOME IS A PLACE
Copyright © 1995 by K.Linda Kivi

1 2 3 4 5 98 97 96 95

The publisher would like to thank the Canada Council, the British Columbia Ministry of Small Business, Tourism and Culture, and the Book Publishing Industry Development Program of the Department of Canadian Heritage for ongoing financial assistance.

Cover design by Jim Brennan
Author photograph by Ronna Bloom
Editing by Julian Ross and Brenda Brooks
Printed in Canada

CANADIAN CATALOGUING IN PUBLICATION DATA
Kivi, K.Linda, 1962-
 If home is a place
 ISBN 1-896095-02-X
 I. Title.
PS8571.I94I4 1995   C813'.54   C95-910724-X
PR9199.3.K58I4 1995

POLESTAR BOOK PUBLISHERS
1011 Commercial Drive
Second Floor
Vancouver, BC
Canada   V5L 3X1
(604) 251-9718

I think, sometimes, that we were children too overshadowed by our parents' stories, and without enough sympathy for ourselves, for the serious dilemmas of our own lives, and who thereby couldn't live up to our parents' desire — amazing in its strength — to create new life and to bestow on us a new world. And who found it hard to learn that in this new world too one must learn all over again, each time from the beginning, the trick of going on.

— Eva Hoffman,
Lost In Translation:
A Life In A New Language

◆ ◆

IF HOME IS A PLACE, HOW DO WE FIND IT? ARE THERE keys dangling, like an extra set of fingers, from your hand? Is there a car idling in a darkened lot waiting to careen down orange lit streets? Or, is there a warm path beneath the pines that calls to the soles of your leathery feet, inviting you to hop over rocks and roots and raise the familiar dust?

Does a breeze stir the grasses, rustle the moonlight in the trees? Is the sun blazing hard enough to shatter shadows?

Can you see home before you get there or is it a surprise, hidden among the trees, only for those who know where to look? Are you greeted by the piled logs of a cabin, the gritty canvas of a tent, a leaning shack or red bricks and a two-car garage?

Who is in the window? What is in the doorway? A cat, a friend, a light, a lover? A spotted begonia, a child, Mamma?

Or are the curtains drawn tight and grim?

Is mail collecting at a windy corner? Are there poppies and petunias to admire as you make your way toward that anticipated something? Or tall trellises of peas, their fragrant flowers transparent and hungry?

Once inside, do your feet fall onto thick pile of carpet or knotted wood? Does the air taste of garlic, oranges, pork roast or that familiar smell people call nothing when what they mean is the fragrance of home? Is there a switch to flick, a knob to turn, or a fire to crouch before and kindle for warmth?

And the people — who are they? Where are they? Do they sing shrill pitches or slam like doors when the wrong questions are asked? Are they people you hide with or from? Is there a hug to be had or does the space only echo solitary silences?

Which way does the bathroom door swing? What colour are the kitchen cupboards? Is there a crack in the bedroom ceiling? What does the poster on the back of the door read? Does the pilot light on the stove need to be relit? Does the mud on the dog's paws matter?

Or did you not get this far? Has home been

supplanted by a shopping mall parking lot, usurped by a monstrous house, enveloped by a troublesome regime or inhabited by ogres?

Is home a place to run to or from? What do you dream there?

We ask and hope for answers.

MARIA ◆ FALL 1943

THE EARTH WARMS MY HANDS. I SCOOP HANDFUL after handful onto the newspaper at my side. Its woody smell, like turnip stew, swells into a hard knot in my throat. It is rich, mole-coloured earth, and even in the dark, I know its colours and will remember its texture. This night, our last before we flee the advancing Russian army, is no time to mark it into my memory. The hole beside me must grow as deep as my biggest cauldron before the moon rises and exposes our hiding place. What is buried cannot be stolen. At least not before we return.

If we return. Helgi picked the hiding spot. "Mamma, *siin*, here. Nobody will know to look here under the pine."

Helgi is my youngest daughter, the quiet one. She squats a few feet away, a vague shadow on the other side of the hole, and digs. The German soldiers took our shovel and left us only a big metal spoon with which to scrape loose the earth. Except for when we strike a stone, the spoon does its work quietly.

The neighbours mustn't hear or they'll come digging for our pots and pans as soon as we are gone. Juhan, my ever-trusting husband, said to leave them be. But he doesn't understand how hungry the people across the border are. He doesn't know how angry Russians have become. Neighbours there are not, "like knots on one loop of string." It was the neighbour who denounced my brother Leoni, my twin. It was only a matter of time before they came for me.

Twenty-two years I have lived in this place. Twenty-two years have passed since I slipped across the line between my old world and this new one. Estonia, Estonia: must I leave you too? I pitch a handful of earth at the pile.

When the Germans crossed the Narva River, pushed the Red Army out of Estonia, back into Russia, Juhan wanted us to leave right away. Away from the Russian border. Away from danger. But where is there no danger? Besides, his mother, Emme, Sofi and Helgi's grandmother, could not feed us all. No. It is enough that she have her son and Sofi, in her little house. And that Helgi is with me.

"How do you feel? Are you warm enough?" I whisper to Helgi and reach for her face. Her cheek is cool and her breathing is steady and strong.

"I'm fine, Mamma," she answers in her small voice. The sanatorium doctors said that the infection has been enclosed in one corner of her lung and that if we take care, feed her well, keep her calm, it won't awaken. But how will we do that away from home?

I cup a handful of soil in my palms. This earth has given and given, fed us our potatoes, cabbage, beets, turnips, parsnips and carrots for so many years. From the bottom corner of the yard, we cut the logs for the house and gathered firewood for the winter. And what have I given in return? A few shovels of manure ladled from the cow and pig pens into the garden every year. And now, my pots and pans.

The big frying pan still smells of pork fat. And somewhere is a faint odour of fish. Is it from my soup cauldron? When we were still young, Leoni and I, not just twins but friends as well, used to fish for perch in the Baltic. And our grandmother would make soup, the peppercorns and bay leaves floating on top as the fish flaked from the bones and sank to the bottom where the potatoes cooked. Fish soup was Leoni's favourite. Juhan's too. He would know what I was cooking the moment he came home from work. With coal dust from the train engines still thick in his mustache, he would ask for a taste. "Only one spoonful," I would say, reaching the spoon up to the open mouth that would later kiss mine, "and then you wash."

My pots. They sit so quietly in the dark. So quietly,

so demurely, that I don't see the two shining yellow eyes next to them until they blink. I wipe the sweat from my upper lip with my apron. It is Nurr, our cat. He meows.

"Shhh." I scold him, but what does he understand?

The volcano of earth on the newspaper beside me is dry. When I squeeze it, I can feel how winter has kissed the soil already. Though it's still warm, its dryness draws the moisture from my hands. Pebbles roll down the sides of the mound. The deeper we dig, the coarser it becomes. The deeper we dig the more voices there are in the air. Old ones. Ones that live in my head.

"Mamma, *mis on?* What is it?" Helgi's voice comes from far away. Then she is quiet to hear what I'm listening for.

Knockknock ... BANGBANGBANG! Atkroite dveer! Open Up! Immediately! Father goes to the door. Does not open it wider than his face. He knows they have come for my twin brother Leoni. Or me. Uniforms. Thick belted at the waist. Red stars on their epaulettes. The heavy odour of tobacco seethes through the door.

They took Leoni, warning me, shaking their grizzled hands, chapped from too many night visits. Father rowed me across the border to Estonia, to here, the next night. That was before the searchlights, police boats, barbed wire and dogs encircled the others who had reason to fear. All these years, living just across the border from them, not even a day's walk away, and ... Twenty five years. I hoped that when the Germans pushed their way to Leningrad, there would be word. But no, all the Russians had been evacuated out of the Germans' way. Gone. Without a trace.

"Mamma." Helgi calls me so quietly that for a moment I'm not sure whether it is her or the wind in the pine that I hear. She calls me again.

"Mamma. There's a rock here. Under the root." I reach into the hole, toward the point in her voice. There, in the place where the raspy root arches out of the ground, I feel the cold of a rock underneath. It's the size of a turnip and resists when I try to wedge it out.

Should we leave it be? "Dig around it," I tell her. "Dig under. I'll try to push it out once it has room to move." The spoon strikes the rock, like a knife being sharpened, rhythmic and fierce.

"Shhhh. Helgi!" She pulls back. She is not used to being scolded. "Just be quiet," I add, more gently.

She begins to dig again and I kneel closer to her side of the hole. I bend into the earth like an Arab praying. How right it seems to pray this way. God, I want to ask, what will happen this time?

The wind runs past, faster now than when we began. It has no answers. The poplars clap their leaves in the dark and the pine showers withered needles onto my head. Nurr sulks silently in the blackness next to my pots and pans. On the rim of the horizon, beyond the house, the sky is becoming silver.

"The moon," I say to my daughter. We've got to work quickly. It won't be long before we are exposed.

A sharp creak nearby. Who is at the gate? Who has heard us? Who has come? I fall still. Helgi stops moving too. Like two rabbits in the dark, we listen.

"Our neighbour," Helgi whispers. Someone's on her back step. It was her door. Footsteps fall on the soft ground. Is it her, going to throw her slop water on her garden, or the tall, German officer who lives in her front room with his assistant? A match strikes flint and I know that it's him, not her. He can't see us through the hedge of lilacs and probably doesn't care about our pots. I breathe again. He has other worries. Two nights ago he came to our door and told us we have to leave. Everyone to the east of the Narva River is being evacuated. Two years ago, we hid from the Soviet evacuation east and now we are being sent west. Armies marching back and forth over our land; what business do they have here? What business do they have sending us away?

I told the Kapten, "Yes, Juhan has already sent for us. We will leave in a few days." And then, when he turned away, his shiny black boots spinning on heel, I told him what they must do with our house when we are gone. "Burn it. Don't leave it for the Bolsheviks." My begonias will freeze anyway. And they won't like the house without us.

The door creaks again. He goes inside and leaves the night air tense. We work again, faster now. Have to sleep well tonight. The walk will be long tomorrow. At least there is still the cow to pull the cart with our potatoes, our things. I go over the list in my head one more time as we scoop soil out of the hole. One dress each besides the ones we are wearing, two sharp knives, two sets of bed linen — Sofi and Juhan took theirs with them to Emme's. One warm coat — Helgi's is too small for her already — mittens, scarves, stockings, underwear. I tucked the silver candlesticks in among our clothes. And the pictures too — I could not leave them behind. Juhan and my wedding picture. One of my parents. The torn one of Leoni, me and our sisters. Bits of Helgi's medicines, our wedding certificate and the Tsar's gold ruble that Father pressed into my hand as I steadied myself, one foot in my new land and the other in the rocking boat. I won it when I was little, only four or five, for buttoning up my coat. Even now I remember how warm it was. He must have been holding it the entire way, wedged between his palm and the oar, as he rowed me to safety. Now, it makes a round lump in my shoe, under my heel.

"Mamma," Helgi's voice startles me. For a moment, it is not hers but some young, forgotten, woman's voice. One of my sisters?

"Is this deep enough. Can we move the rock?" she asks. I put my foot in the hole against the rock and brace myself on a root and push. It gives easily and Helgi lifts it out and staggers away with it into the alder bush like a modern day Linda. Thirteen and so tall already. When they were little, the girls never tired of Juhan's stories about the Estonian mythic hero, and his mother, Linda, who in her sorrow over her husband's death, carried an enormous boulder until she could no longer, then sat upon it to cry. She cried a lake of loss to forever remind her descendants of her tale.

I press my heavy iron cauldron into the hole. The cauldron will hold all the other pots. It doesn't quite fit. *Kurat!* The gap between the root and the floor of our pit is not quite high enough. I wiggle the cauldron back out from under the root and take the spoon from where Helgi left it and scrape some more. There is no time to lose. The moon is already half above the trees and soon the pine will no longer shadow us.

Helgi comes back to the hole and stands beside me awkwardly, listening to the nightbirds, the nightingale and owl, calling the moon up from its sleep. She thinks that I can't hear her crying. Does she think that tears can worry me? Does she think that we have time to mope about, like cows who have lost their calves?

"Helgi, come," I say to her. "Let's try it again." The big pot fits this time. Like a thread through a needle. We tug the cauldron out again and put the other pots inside, like wooden Russian dolls, from the largest to the smallest. Helgi pads the spaces between with old hay that crumbles in her hands. One at a time and quietly, I put the pots in. Finally, I put the frying pan on top and lower it into the ground.

Helgi and I fill the rest of the hole. A few pebbles ping against the metal sides but the rising wind masks our little noises. The musk of the soil fills my head and once again I swallow hard, as if something is stuck in my throat. I breathe in and out carefully, as if to measure the air while we fill the hole. We pat the earth down as we go.

Once the hole is almost filled I think about my cutlery. I can't take it. It isn't silver. But I can't leave it either — Juhan's brother made it for him before he died.

"Wait," I tell Helgi, "go get the cutlery." She runs toward the house and, as she goes inside, the moon finally slips out from behind the pine. It seems like a new moon, one that I don't know, so much brighter than the old one. If someone were to come down the road now, they would see us, fugitives in a spotlight. But the road is quiet.

Helgi leaves the back door ajar. What if it slams shut? I get up from my knees — they are stiff — and go prop the door open with a log. The glow of the kerosene lamp shines from the front room but I don't hear Helgi. Perhaps she is dreaming again or transfixed by the mirror. Ever since she was a little girl, she would ask Juhan to lift her up so that she could look into it and touch the gilt frame. She would run her fingers, which were thin even then, over the oak leaves that were carved into the wood, or she would simply look at her own reflection, with the curiosity of a chicken that has found a spoon.

When I step into the front room, she turns and smiles at me. She has opened the two top drawers of the sideboard and is taking each piece out, one by one, placing them on top among my spotted begonias.

How can I scold such a gentle child?

"*Tule laps,* Come child." I fill both my hands with the forks, spoons, knives and serving pieces that are wrapped in old dress rags. Helgi does the same. We walk quickly back to the hole, Nurr running in front of our feet.

I take the half-buried frying pan off the top and we squeeze the cutlery into the smallest pot. The ladle doesn't fit. I try to push it down the side, between the cauldron and the big pot but the bowl still sticks out. I try another place. And then another.

Helgi takes my hand by the wrist suddenly. "Give," she says, and carries it away, toward the back of the yard, through the half light.

"I buried it in its own hole, a secret place," she tells me when she comes back.

"But how will I find it?" I ask her.

"I'll find it for you. It's in its own nest." We fill our hole. We smooth the earth over our spot. We scatter needles over it and brush our footprints away with a frond of the pine. We hurry back into the house with the blank windows. Tomorrow morning, we go away from the front. To join Sofi and Juhan at Emme's.

◆ SUMMER 1988

ESTHER LOOKED UP FROM THE SINK, OUT THE window. Her nephews were twisting and squealing, their twenty plump fingers fluttering like so many eager birds. Elmar, Esther's father, their grandfather, was stirring dish soap and water in a plastic bucket using a stick from the apple tree. It was time to blow bubbles, their favourite distraction.

Elmar blew the first bubble; it shimmered across the low wire fence that divided Esther's parents' yard from the neighbours and burst. Howls of "me next, me next!", the perpetual cry of siblings close in age, rang out.

Esther lifted a handful of cutlery out of the greying water beneath the froth. With her mother Sofi outside,

Esther could linger over her Sunday evening task. As she slid the dish rag across each spoon, fork and knife, they caught glints of the autumn evening sun that sloped in the kitchen window. A bit of beauty, a bit of peace.

Outside, Elmar was busy bringing the boys various dipping devices, two at a time, from his workshop at the back of the garage. Sometimes her quiet father surprised her with his imaginativeness: a scissors' handle created a two-in-one effect and the disembodied buttocks and breasts floated off across the lawn; the funnel that the boys fought over, because you could blow directly into it and there was only one, produced huge wobbly bubbles that quickly snapped; a sprocket set filled the air with a solar system of dusky globes that seemed to wander throughout the yard before they lost their lives to the apple tree, or against the sharp stucco of the house.

At the edge of their commotion, Sofi, who was usually in charge, seemed at a loss for what to do. Her camera dangled forlornly from her wrist, as if she had lost all hope of snapping the boys into stillness. Occasionally, she pointed out a bubble that was rising quickly or one that slipped among the branches of the apple tree without bursting, but the only ones who paid attention were Aunt Helgi and Maria, *Vanaema*, Esther's grandmother.

Helgi and Vanaema, daughter and mother, watched from the safety of the patio, Helgi in her characteristic stance, lanky arms folded around her midriff, one long leg extended as if to balance her tall frame. Vanaema, Esther's unchanging mouse of a grand-mother, sat in a lawn chair, small eyes blinking behind her round, wire-frame glasses. Esther smiled to herself, pulled her wrinkled hands out of the suds and wiped them on her jeans.

The pots now. With the kitchen to herself, Esther enjoyed doing dishes.

Sofi had given up her usual task of drying and telling Esther in what order to wash the dishes (as if she didn't know already from years of being instructed in the "wifely arts") in order to be where the action was.

"Glasses first. Then the coffee cups. Bowls, plates, serving dishes, cutlery and the pots last," she reminded Esther, in Estonian, as she rushed out the back door. "And don't you forget to rinse — the cutlery especially."

"Don't worry, I will … forget," she'd muttered the final word, a concession to herself, as the spring on the back door gave its characteristic howl.

How had that hinge escaped Sofi, Elmar's oiling can? Who had given it permission to screech?

The kitchen window framed the family scene as well as any television could. Sofi liked that. She was happiest when everyone was clustered around her dining room table, eating and being within her sight. The only blot on the day had been Bob's absence. Kadri, Esther's sister, had excused her husband's absence. Work, she said. Bob was always working.

Esther suspected that her parents appreciated his

absence. When Bob wasn't around, they spoke in Estonian even though the twins didn't understand. Though Vanaema was used to being excluded — she had never learned English — Esther liked it when they included her. It wasn't that Vanaema ever complained; she just sat quietly, eating like a bird and tapping Helgi or Esther's hand if she wanted anything, which she rarely did. Occasionally, Sofi would take notice of her mother, in the way she took notice of things or people, completely and utterly, leaving them nowhere to hide.

"*Mamma, Söö*, Eat!" she had exclaimed at dinner and lifted another helping of potatoes, roast pork and sauerkraut onto Vanaema's plate, ignoring the fact that she would, when Sofi's attention shifted back to the boys, scoop everything onto Helgi or Esther's plate. Vanaema could not bear to leave anything. And Esther, even at twenty-five, would be scolded if she did. Inevitably, Esther would end up feeling bloated and slightly nauseous on Sunday nights.

Esther scraped the remains of the sauerkraut into a plastic container and pressed the second-to-last pot into the sink, letting the water cascade over the sides gradually, until it filled and disappeared. Drowned. Like her peas. They'd been having trouble with the water timer in the greenhouse; last weekend it hadn't turned itself off. When she came in on Monday morning, she found her first round of experimental pea beds bobbing in five centimetres of water. Things could be better, Esther thought.

As if her master's research wasn't trouble enough, over dinner Sofi had launched into her usual rant. "When are you going to find someone ..." blah, blah, "... time to settle ..." blah, blah, and then, a new twist: "There's a nice little house on Inkster. We'd help you with the downpayment ..."

Sofi had it all worked out. She'd even been to see the house, measured the rooms, calculated what furniture Esther could take out of their basement. In her mind, Sofi had painted the walls, had Elmar rebuild the bathroom, put a kitchenette, toilet and shower stall in the basement and ... "You could pay the mortage with the rent money from downstairs. Or at least most of it."

The squeal of the back door interrupted Esther's thoughts. Helgi pulled a tea towel off the oven door handle and dislodged a plate from the back of the precarious pile.

"You shouldn't let Sofi get to you," Helgi began, as if she had been following Esther's thoughts all along, from outside.

"I'm used to it," Esther shrugged. "You'd think that after all these years she'd give up trying to boss me around."

Helgi shook her head and smiled.

"No, really. When have I ever done what she's wanted?" Esther wondered out loud.

"That isn't why she does it."

"Your grant money would cover the rest," Esther mimicked Sofi, "I mean, you pay rent anyway." She turned toward Helgi, her eyes big and maniacal to emphasize the point.

Helgi chuckled. "Just remember, I've been her sister for my entire life. She's got a good heart."

There was no denying that. Esther's parents had always been eager to give as much as they could. They helped her set up house — or rather room — when she left home to go to university. Not only had they let her take all her bedroom furniture, but Sofi had found her an almost complete set of stainless steel pots and pans at a yard sale and provided a selection of mis-matched plates and bowls.

On moving day, when everything had been carried in, her mother produced a small jar of instant coffee, a tupperware cup of milk and a half dozen of the sugar packets that her father collected every time they ate in a restaurant. Esther had plugged the kettle in and put one spoonful of coffee in each mug; they could do the rest. When she sat back down at the green formica kitchen table, Sofi had laid out a complete set of cutlery for four. New.

"Your housewarming present. If you don't like them, I can't return them, they were on sale. But if you want more, let me know because they might be on sale again and then we can complete the set. You'll need twelve all together."

"Thanks, Mamma." Esther didn't need more than four. Just more to lose track of. It wasn't as though she was going to be throwing dinner parties. Half of her high school friends had moved away from

Winnipeg to go to University. Besides, she wouldn't have any time. All those years, seven and a half since then, and she still had the original set of four, minus two knives that housemates had blackened smoking hash.

Elmar had sat quietly that day, as he usually did, not quite present and not quite absent. When Esther came back in after seeing them out to the car, her mother clutching her in a teary farewell, she had discovered his present on the table. A set of wooden spoons and a spatula. Esther had rubbed them in her hands, pulling their smooth grain across her palms, swirling her thumbs in the perfect hollow of the spoons. He had carved them himself.

Esther had the only set of her father's spoons. Shortly after, the twins were born and Elmar usurped Helgi's traditional role as the provider of surprises and toys. His workshop began to produce wooden mobiles, building blocks, cars and planes with moveable parts, miniature furniture. Everything in pairs, almost identical but always with some little twist so that they could be told apart. The toys, like the spoons, were indestructible.

Esther tipped the roasting pan into the water. Sofi had already poured the drippings into a jar she kept in the refrigerator.

"So what about the house?" Helgi interrupted her reverie.

"Not you too."

"This time she's right, Esther. Why spend money

on rent when you could be making an investment." Helgi's sudden shift to her bookkeeper voice surprised Esther.

"Since when have I been interested in investments? Since when have you been interested in investments? *Tädi Helgi*, really." Esther's childhood "Auntie Helgi" came out of her mouth without a thought. She had stopped calling her that years ago.

"I don't need to argue with you, Esther. You know me better than that. Think about it."

Esther didn't want to think about it and avoided the corner of her brain where the suggestion lodged, like a patriarch in an overstuffed armchair, for the rest of the evening. The boys came back inside as the fall evening darkened and cooled. Sofi bustled around the kitchen, putting the coffee to perk, arranging cups, saucers and the tiny coffee spoons on a tray; Sunday night was their only break from instant.

"Thanks for doing the dishes," she patted Esther's shoulder. "Would you mind getting the cheesecake, please? It's in the downstairs fridge."

Esther descended the stairs slowly. She loved the old fridge, the way you had to yank the handle to get it open, the musty smell and the labels: fruit, vegetables and meat on the metal crispers. Sofi had always followed their lead and often complained that there was no drawer for cheese, as if one of the others wouldn't do. Nothing ever got thrown away in her parents' house. Esther caught herself thinking — maybe they'll give me the fridge if I buy a house.

No, she wasn't buying a house. She didn't want a house. At least not in Winnipeg.

She pulled the lever handle and the light switched on. A cottage cheesecake. Her favourite. In the big rectangular glass pan. As always. The moist fragrance of lemon wafted upward. The crust would be flecked with yellow from the peel, the filling wet and tart. She inhaled deeply all the way upstairs, even after Sofi called out to see what was keeping her so long.

At the table, the boys insisted on having fruit on top, "like real cheese cake," though Kadri tried to tell them this was a different kind. The dollop of raspberry jam that Sofi indulged them with seemed to satisfy their six-year-old sense of correctness. The boys made a mush of the red and creamy white, nibbled at the edges of the crust and left the rest.

Sofi would finish the leftovers after everyone was gone, patting the round belly that every woman her age had, complaining about getting fat. Elmar would say, predictably, "then don't eat." And Sofi would eye him maliciously, with a "don't-be-ridiculous" look, of course she had to eat everyone's leftovers. At least Esther would be long gone by then.

After the bustle of everyone finding their coats, the twins stood still as Vanaema planted a slow kiss on the top of each of her great-grandson's heads, as if the solemnity of the gesture could protect them from evils unknown. Everyone spilled out of the front hall onto the lawn to watch Kadri pile her horde into the Volvo. Helgi and Vanaema, who lived together a few kilometres from Sofi's, left with less pomp in an old Buick that was still gold in the places it hadn't rusted. They dropped Esther off at a bus stop.

The street corner was bare, the road empty too. The faces of houses, identical except for the outrageous colours of their wooden fronts, stared at her as if to say "so?" Why did she need a house? If you didn't have anything, then nobody could take it away. Besides, Kadri had a house. She didn't need to be hemmed in, too. She didn't want a house. She had a home, didn't she?

Of course, Sofi wanted a tall man with a profession, a Tory preferably, for her younger daughter too. Sofi. Esther shook her head imperceptibly whenever she thought of her mother. It was Kadri who had started calling their parents by their first names, though not to their faces, when she was a defiant teenager and Esther had thought of her parents as Sofi and Elmar ever since; it made them seem less powerful.

A lone car idled down the street and she stepped out onto the pavement behind it to peer down the long alley of trees. Buses were notoriously tardy on Sunday evenings and it was often a half hour before one came burping and grizzling down the street. She pulled her jean jacket tight around her. The houses stared.

Sometimes, on the wet or wintery days of her childhood, she would pad down the stairs in her slippers to Sofi's sewing room and ask her about home. What was it like? Tell me about your house. What toys did you have? Who did you play with? Was there as much snow as in Winnipeg? Was it flat? What did you grow?

Sofi was best at answering questions about what people wore, who the neighbours were, about goings on, though she'd usually end up on a diatribe about the evils of Communism, of Russians. "Did you know," she would begin, "that Stalin ordered the excecution and deportation of over 100,000 Estonians!?" Of course Esther knew. Who was Sofi reciting these statistics for? And there was no stopping her once she began. The one time that Esther tried to argue the possible merits of the idea of socialism convinced her not to try again. The war was a safer subject, somehow free of politics. That was the exciting part.

"Nothing," she would say, "even if you added up everything that's happened all these years since the war, was as exciting as those years." This was one point that Sofi and Elmar agreed on.

Vanaema, on the other hand, liked to talk about Estonia. Even though she confused details more and more as she got older — an acacia bush suddenly bloomed purple with lilacs, the Baltic moved in and out of earshot — her small eyes lit up and sparkled when she talked about the "old country". And she never joined in on the rants about Russia.

The low rumble of the bus in the distance snapped Esther to attention. Esther's fare tinkled into the box; she was the only passenger. She slumped onto a worn vinyl seat and watched the rows of houses speed past.

Who lived in these places, these lines of stucco and wood houses that perched on quilted pieces of earth? Were these places *home* to all those Ukrainians, Poles and other misplaced human beings who lived in them? Or could they live here because there was the memory of another home, magnificently embellished by over forty-five years of closely tended reminiscenses and sheltered by familiar ghosts somewhere far away?

Her family's stories and those of their friends, essentially fairy tales, were all Esther had; she had never plunged her hands into the legendary soil of Estonia. And what chance was there that she ever would? Esther's childhood battles with her parents were based on the reality of the Soviet Union; it was too huge, it would never budge. "But precisely," Sofi would state, intransigent in her certitude, "that is why we need to keep our culture alive. We, in the free world." At this juncture, she'd often switch to English; the slogans were, after all, for those with power. They sounded like the placards they had carried when Sofi had taken the girls to protest Kosygin's or Breshnev's visits to Canada. "We need to resist assimilation. Stop Russification. Free the Baltics Now."

But somehow, in spite of Esther's stubborn defiance of Sofi's agenda, her parents' patriotism had sunk in along with an intangible feeling of caution. Esther had come to believe that it was important not to stand out, not to ask for much, not to inspire the greed and lust of the world's ogres. Esther's version of not too much was a careful room at the end of a corridor, a place to shelve her books and a window for her spider plant to bask. A place that would hopefully remain beyond the covetous glances of urban developers. She, like other renters, had repeatedly been swept out, like so many June bugs, when real estate sky-rocketed and the selling season came.

She had moved often since that day when her parents left the fan of cutlery, metal and wooden, on the formica.

She was weary from moving. Was it time to want more of life? If so, what? Esther clung to the top of the seat as the bus swung wide around a corner. After a long, straight stretch she was home, or at least at the house she lived in with four housemates. Women this time around. There was at least one advantage to this; none of them left a spray of beard hairs like an abstract etching around the bathroom sink. And she and Brenda, the other student in the house, were getting to know each other.

At her stop, Esther stepped out onto the sidewalk in front of a newspaper box. The front page photo was of a harvester at work. Then, a name caught her eye. In the side story, down the right side of the page was the headline, curious and unlikely: "Gorbachev Announces Opening." Of what? Another space centre? The cutline read: "Can reconstruction succeed in a society of absolutes?" She crouched down, moving to one side to let the street light illuminate the page through the scratched plexiglass.

It wasn't quite clear what they were talking about. There was a string of political words: perestroika, glasnost, liberalization. She scanned the article to the bottom where "continued page 6" halted her mid-sentence. She couldn't imagine what Gorbachev really meant. Communism was communism, wasn't it? More rhetoric. Did he think that history could be altered with the utterance of a few slippery Russian words?

Esther eyed the article skeptically. Her parents would dismiss any hope of change. They'd say it was a scam to lure the resistance out from underground. Their family had followed the few protests of the past years where, when the moles had come up for air, it was only to discover that they were bound to be flattened under the giant's footsteps.

Esther patted her pockets, looking for change. None. Oh well. It probably wasn't worth reading anyway. Some things never change.

The verandah light cast green shadows through the foliage of the tremendous elm in the front yard of the lanky wooden house. She looked up into it, noticing that the veins of the leaves were yellowing, as if they were eating what was left of the summer sun. It was quiet except for their rustling. Esther shivered. Home at last.

The house was quiet. She stepped in, closing the door behind her. Softly, she climbed the wooden stairs to her room under the eaves.

HELGI ◆ SEPTEMBER 1944

I WAKE SUDDENLY FROM A DREAM EXPECTING TO find Nurr, my cat from home, at my feet. But no, this is my grandmother Emme's house in Rakvere. Rakvere now. I must have fallen asleep when Emme was here in the night. She often comes to me when I can't sleep. How does she know that I'm awake when her room is downstairs, next to the kitchen? Even Isa, my father, and Mamma, whose bed is in the other room under the eaves, our two doors yawning at each other sleepily, never hear me squirm. Mamma sleeps there alone now that Isa has gone to join the Homeguard. And of course Sofi, who breathes heavily on the other side of our dark room, doesn't notice me either. She's dead like a winter bear until breakfast is already cooking.

I sit up and pull the quilt up under my nose. The house is completely quiet, completely still. Will Emme come again? Or is it morning already?

When Emme comes up the creaking stairs, she brings me warm milk and honey — *soe piim ja mesi.* I know that when she stops on the landing halfway up to catch her breath, she will soon be in my doorway. She pauses there too, backlit by the *tattnina* — the snotnose — the tiny kerosene lamp that lives on the landing where it is lit every night so that wanderers can find their road back to bed. Mamma says Emme has asthma. Sometimes her breath is so heavy that I'm afraid it won't rise up out of her.

Miks sa ei maga, "Why aren't you asleep," Emme asked when she came into my room. "Did *Unematti* throw all his sleepdust at your sister again? Doesn't he see you here every night, not closing your eyes?"

We laughed gently at Sofi, as we often do, who is such a Snow White, except that her prince is the coffee genie who sneaks up the stairs to wake her every morning. It's only grain coffee now, but it still plucks her out of those noisy dreams of hers which she says she doesn't remember. She has to get up early, even before the sky is pink, to go work at the hospital caring for the soldiers. She says she wants to be a nurse. But mostly she wants a husband. That's all she ever talks about.

I always remember my dreams. I tell Emme about them when she comes to me. What was the dream that I just woke up from? I lie back down and close my eyes to remember it better. It was about Nurr. Where is my grey striped Nurr now? Has he gone to sleep on another girl's bed? Or have all the girls run away too?

In my dream Nurr was meowing on some stairs, stairs like a rainbow, each step a different colour. He wanted me to go up with him. I could hear the wind blowing but I wasn't sure where it was. I looked behind me and saw a grey door with a window. I went and looked and saw only a big grey field with trees all around it, swaying madly in the wind and my father, Isa, walking away. Only in the dream his thick hair was white and his high shoulders were stooped. A gun hung from his shoulder, across his back. He did not see me. I turned away and went toward Nurr. He kept a couple of steps ahead of me, half purring, half meowing, saying that he wanted me to come with him. I went up and up but awoke before I got to the top.

I throw the quilt off and put my warm feet on the cold floor. Emme hasn't yet heard me so it must be morning. Sunday: not even Mamma is up. I'm the first. The steps creak as I go downstairs, singing to me the same way that they do when Emme comes up in the middle of the night.

On the landing where Emme always pauses is an eye, an oval window as big as my face and just the right height. I look out of it into our yard every morning. The plum and apple trees seem like monsters in the shadows, if you don't know what they really are. It's too dark to see the fruit so I turn the *tattnina* off. Its glass bulb glows for a second yet and then is dark. My eyes take a moment to adjust. The smooth oak table where the tattnina sits, more like a spindly stool than a table, emerges from the darkness first.

Outside, the sky is getting brighter — and the frost is outlined by the rosy light. It's early for frost, the grass hasn't even yellowed but oh, the apples will be sweet now. The trees are laced silvery and magical. All the world is still, except for me. Nobody here but me and the sun who has just given the roofs of Rakvere their first morning kiss. One ray touches the chicken house wall. It won't be long before the rooster's *kokorikoo!* wakes Emme. Emme's chickens are rust-coloured. Before the soldiers came and butchered them, our chickens at home were brownish and small, but the eggs tasted just the same.

I creak the rest of the way down into the kitchen, stepping as carefully as I can. At the bottom, I tiptoe past Emme's open door into the front room on the other side of the kitchen. The sun has yawned a tall yellow stripe across the oak floor. A good place to stand.

The wood has begun to warm and my toes are happy on the waxy floor even if the rest of me is chicken skin. Mamma would scold me if she saw me here without my stockings, my slippers and my cardigan. Emme would only pull me into the Deep Chair and ask whether the elves had eaten the sweater she knit for me when I first came to Emme's a year ago. My dear old coat with the lambskin collar and cuffs was too small, or I was too big, and we had to leave it at home. We had to leave so much behind and now, there are no coats or boots or anything to buy anywhere.

But what do I need with boots when I am in Emme's house? There is the Deep Chair to curl up in. Its green and yellow vines surround me as I snuggle into a wool blanket the colour of the sky. The blanket lives on the arm of the chair. Can I reach it without stepping off the sun? I walk with my hands until I'm stretched out to my full 163 centimetres (almost 164!) but even though I'm taller than Emme, Mamma and Sofi, I still can't reach it. Isa could. I don't think I'll ever catch up to him; the top of my head still only comes to his chin. I think Mamma is shrinking, though Sofi tells me not to be stupid, that it's me that is growing.

One step off the stripe — the floor is cold — and I reach, reach, reach until I catch hold of one corner of the blanket. Warm, nice. A picture of Isa's brother smiles from the sideboard. Emme showed me pictures of him and Isa when they were little boys. When I asked where Isa's brother was, Emme cried in my hair, said that there was another war before this one.

It was true, they had talked about it in school but I heard only the end of it. I must have been in the sanatorium for the rest. They didn't make us go to classes there. It was important to rest.

I am still standing on my piece of sun, though it has moved and me with it, when Emme wakes up and comes to find me wrapped up in her beautiful blanket like an Indian.

"*Paljad jalad!* Bare feet! Don't let your mother see you. Here. Take my slippers. I'll go get my other ones." She slides her slippers in front of me and I put them on. They are too short and my heels hang out over the backs but they are as warm as pancakes.

From the kitchen comes the crackling of lit kindling and the muffled clatter of pots as Emme starts breakfast. Mamma and Sofi will be down soon and the world will become its bad self again. Every morning now for six days Emme has made pancakes, my favourite breakfast, a goodbye breakfast, though she doesn't say so. I hear Mamma's voice, scolding Emme, telling her not to use up her flour ration on us, but Emme doesn't listen. We'll eat them with the lingonberry jam that Emme and I made last September when Mamma and I first came to her house.

The day we made the jam, there were so many bees, buzzing at the windows, throwing themselves onto the wooden spoon, sticky with red juice and jam. They were crazy and Isa too. He kept coming in from the garden where he was putting a lock on the cow shed, to ask if our jam was ready to be eaten yet.

"Go away," Emme said to him as though he was a little boy. And he went back to his work.

He didn't obey so easily though when we said that we were going to pick mushrooms and berries in the bog.

"You can't go alone," he said, rubbing his long fingers. "You don't know who is hiding in the woods anymore or how desperate they are."

Emme decided that he would come with us. He helped us pick. There are no berries as lovely as lingonberries, the way they hang onto their long stems, like lilies of the valley, but bright, happy red. There were cranberries too but I picked only lingonberries. In the moss, so thick and soft, I picked all around me before moving to another spot. A day to return to.

My sun stripe has moved again, started to climb the wall, and I hear Emme's whisk throw air into the batter. My mouth waters with the first splash of batter on the frying pan. Maybe Emme will let me flip the pancakes; Mamma never wanted me in her kitchen, said we couldn't afford to spoil food, but Sofi complained that she was only doting on me. And then after breakfast Emme will give me my reading and writing lesson. I already know all of the alphabet. The Germans use the same one as ours but their words are different, all except a few ones, like *kohver*, suitcase. Mamma says we'll have to pack ours soon.

I turn around three times quickly, with my arms stretched out from my sides. The blanket swirls as I spin and on the last turn, I let it fly. It flutters to the ground like an enormous, sad blue bird. I gather it up, lay it back across the arm of the Deep Chair and head upstairs to get dressed.

Is this the day that I say goodbye to Emme?

THE HOUSE WAS DARK, BUT WHICH HOUSE WAS THIS? Esther had to think for a few seconds before it came to her. What had she been dreaming? Something about an enormous house, something about the colour blue, an Estonian cornflower blue, full of the sun. It was strange. She didn't usually dream in colours, or if she did, she never remembered what they were. In spite of the blue, there was something disturbing about this house — it was more a sense than a clear image. Esther reached to remember, to peer around the corners in her mind, to capture the fleeing picture.

Were parts of it missing? Was the garden full of insects? Was there someone else in the house?

And there, in the corner of her eye, she caught the

rush of darkness, thick as fur. Footsteps pounding, marching, familiar. No. They couldn't trap her. She ran, the house behind her. The woods full of hungry eyes. Wake up!

She rolled back into a ball. Phew. The quick patter of her heart told her she wouldn't be able to fall asleep again. A cliché lodged in her mind: today is the first day of the rest of her life. The thesis was defended and passed. What now? She rubbed the indent between her breasts as if to draw out an old ache and rolled toward the window. The horizon was pale, a fragile violet-blue like the cracked robin's eggs she used to find under her parents' apple tree. As a child, this time of morning had always frightened her, because she often had nightmares, people running, always pursuit. In the dark there was no way to know it wasn't real. No light to chase away the lingering images, the feeling. At least at home, if she couldn't fall asleep again, she'd crawl into bed with Kadri.

No one to crawl into bed with here, but it wasn't too early to get up. Make breakfast. Read the paper for once.

She swung her legs out from under her thick duvet and sighed. She sighed as deeply as she knew how as if she could expel the dream, the panic, the sense that something impossible was wanted of her. The wood was cool beneath her soles as she stepped toward the closet door, over the fat novels and notebooks she had left sprawled across the floor from a late night of reading and scribbling.

The morning seemed to stretch and yawn as she did, encouraging the hum of city traffic which had already begun. She pulled her jeans on, reached for a pair of the fat woolen socks Sofi knit for her, and pulled them up over the cuffs of her pants. Sofi knitted while watching Lawrence Welk reruns of Sissy and Bobby dancing, always smiling.

She pulled her favourite green t-shirt on, the one with the huge hand-painted purple eggplant on it, and then a sweatshirt. The house was cool, but never cold. She liked that about old houses with wooden floors. They embraced what warmth could be withheld from the blasting prairie weather by huddling close together under a high ceiling of trees.

Sofi's houses, the ones described and pictured in the real estate ads she brought for Esther, rarely had good trees, or a garden. And what was a house without a garden? Esther would ask her as she handed back the sheets, one by one, not finding anything to hold her in any of them. And though Sofi had finally got the message and stopped saving ads to show Esther on Sunday nights, Esther did not let on that the seed, the idea of having a more permanent place to call home, had planted itself in her brain.

But though the seed was planted, there was still the leap that Esther hadn't quite accomplished: how did you make home from a house? That it had to be palpable, wood and stucco and soil and trees was undeniable. But how would it look? Where would it be? This question wasn't new to Esther. The idea of what home looked like had preoccupied her from the moment one bespeckled school teacher handed her a paintbrush and milky pots of blue, red and yellow.

While her sister Kadri painted murky underwater scenes worthy of Rorschach interpretations, she brushed lines and angles, doors and windows onto curling slabs of paper. Then the trees, the bushes, perhaps a fence, a shed or the elusive sauna both her parents claimed they had had. And always a garden, with a splatter of red tomatoes, fat streaks of green that were meant to be cucumbers, a mess of darker green for the potatoes. There was one house, a four story monstrosity with beds scribbled in under the eaves, that Sofi liked so much she had it framed and hung in the rec room. And that was only one attempt.

Esther remembered the frustration of never quite finding it, the definitive place where she would belong. Of trying again and again, over the suburban years of her childhood, to capture something essential, something missing, something longed for, that she could not properly draw. Her crumpled mistakes would pile up around her chair until she abandoned her Laurentian pencils and went to search for shiny turquoise bugs in the garden.

Esther pulled a second sweatshirt on and tiptoed past the two other bedrooms on her floor. She carefully stepped over the step with a creak. No point in waking the others.

At the bottom of the stairs, Esther pulled the front door open and the paper slumped in, like a dead body someone had propped between the doors.

She carried the fat sheaf of newsprint into the kitchen and laid it flat on the table.

She turned on the kitchen light and filled the kettle. She scooped coffee into the filter. What did she want? No, not cereal. Not granola. She wanted something else, something comfortingly familiar yet not boringly usual. She smacked her lips, reaching to taste a lingering flavour that did not want to give itself away. Pancakes. Yes, pancakes. Maybe Brenda would have some with her if she got up soon. She had flour, she could borrow some baking powder.

She opened the fridge and pulled the quart of milk and a half dozen eggs from her quarter of the dark hole. When Elmar had seen that they had no light in the fridge during one of his rare visits, he had taken the bulb and bought her a new one. It didn't work either.

She plunked the ingredients on the table next to the paper. Esther had started to read newpapers again when the Soviet Union began making headlines on a regular basis. There were even dribs and drabs about the Baltic states and the protests that had begun to erupt there. Esther followed the news, as did her parents, their friends, and even Helgi and Kadri, though everyone did it with such true Estonian trepidation that you'd hardly know that they were paying attention. People from diminutive countries were like that. You stayed quiet in hopes that nobody would notice your presence, like a mouse going about its business while the cats sat on table tops licking clean their paws.

The gleaming eyes in the dream. Esther blinked. No. They were not cat-like.

Esther cracked the brown shell of the egg against the bowl, releasing the deep yellow inside. She loved eggs. Bought the best kind — farm fresh, range fed, organic. It wasn't that she was much of a health food buff, but she loved the glow of their dark yolks and the way their flavour burst slowly and gently.

She pursued the front page while beating the eggs to a froth. November 17: almost winter and she'd done nothing about her future yet. Her supervisor had handed her a few names and addresses, professors at different schools around the continent to contact. He wanted her to do her PhD. She hadn't written to anyone. It had been months and she had felt as though she were waiting, though for what, she couldn't quite decide. Just waiting for some kind of magical unfolding that would reveal the stone inside the fruit.

Esther scanned the front page for news about the Eastern Bloc. So much was happening there that events had to be monumental, or at least violent, to make the front page. Estonia was too little to be monumental and too polite to be violent.

Esther ladled three streams of pale yellow batter onto the hot pan, lifting the excess back into the bowl, leaving a trail of droplets between it and the stove.

Leafing the pages casually, she scanned the local and regional news without absorbing much. To turn to the international pages without a passing glance over the rest was somehow risky, as if her eagerness could bring about tragedy.

She scooped the first three cakes onto a plate and slipped them into the warm oven. She cooked the rest of the pancakes in silence, sipping milky coffee while she made a shopping list. She had been promising herself a good load of groceries for months now but school, or dinner with Helgi and Vanaema, or something, always stood in the way.

Herring. She never bought herring. Previous roommates had found its odour repugnant, especially if she smothered it in sour cream.

Sour Cream. She wrote everything down with capitals. What else? She realized that she wanted *Pirukad, Rasolje*, coldcuts and Polish cow candies. *Sült*, which she loved as long as she didn't think of it as headcheese, cloudberry jam, *Scumbria* in its tomatoey sauce, and Roonem Bakery's special recipe sweet and sour rye bread. Stuff that was hard to get in Winnipeg if you could get it at all. When Sofi and Elmar's friends came from Toronto, they'd bring an extra suitcase, loaded so full of bread from the Estonian bakery that her father could barely lift it. And squirreled in among their clothes might be a jar of lingonberry sauce or bag of hard gingerbread cookies.

There weren't enough Estonians, or even Latvians and Estonians combined, to merit a delicatessen in Winnipeg. Toronto was a different story.

She piled the last three pancakes into the oven and

went to the bottom of the stairs. She could hear her housemate's clock radio blarring. She raised her head to shout and then didn't. Brenda would come down when she was ready.

Maybe Esther should move to Toronto. She had plenty of friends there, garnered over the years of visits and the two summers that Sofi had sent her and Kadri to a summer camp north of the city. She'd kept in touch with a few: wild Maret, who never quite measured up in Sofi's eyes because her father wasn't Estonian, quiet Kristiina who was her most faithful correspondent and Kalev, who, when the spirit moved him, which was only fitfully and with bizarre twists, would court her.

Esther twirled her Estonian ring around her finger, feeling the ridges of oak leaves and the flat plate of the coat of arms. Blue for the sky, black for the rich earth and white for the purity of the Estonian heart — that was one version at least. Others waxed less lyrical and said that the white represented birch trees. Or snow. What she never understood was why there were lions on the coat of arms. Where did a bunch of lowland, northern peasants find out about lions?

Esther pulled the warm plate out of the oven and let the springed oven door slam shut. If her housemates weren't awake before, they were now. No, she thought, as the kitchen chair let out a hiss of air, she didn't want to move to Toronto. It would just be more of the same. The same what? That was what she couldn't quite grasp. She filled her plate with pancakes and began to eat just as the phone rang.

It was Helgi. She was calling to invite her niece for dinner. To talk. "What if I don't have anything to talk about? Do you still want me?" Her family couldn't bear to watch her in limbo. Even Helgi had taken to questioning her, urging her to act.

"We always want you. Vanaema's making pirukad today. And borscht. She sometimes forgets about the stove," Helgi added in English.

"Sure." What else was there to do? "Put Vanaema on."

"Es-ter?" Vanaema's voice rose thinly across the phonelines. "*Oled tark tüdruk.* Your peas are better than the ones I buy in the grocery store. Be a good girl."

"I'm coming for dinner Vanaema."

"*Jah, jah*, good peas. Good peas." Vanaema had never quite grasped that Esther grew peas for research, not for market.

"*Äiteh Vanaema.* Bye," she said in English and hung up abruptly.

Vanaema never liked the phone. If no one else was at home to answer it, Vanaema would pick the receiver up and listen to find out who was being asked for. For a time, it was usually Kadri. "Kadri not home!" Vanaema would shout into the receiver and slam it back down. Kadri would be furious when her friends would ask her who the grouch at her house was. But what else could she do?

Esther sat back down, speared a hunk of pancake,

put it in her mouth and peered at the paper on her left.

Finally, the international page. Oh my God. *Estonian Soviet Republic declares Sovereignty*, the headline read.

Shit. Her mouth went dry. That was really tempting the bastards. The lump of half-chewed pancake felt like a dry sponge in her mouth. She gulped it down with some coffee and read the cutline: *Soviet parliament overrules.*

What else had they done? As she read the article and realized that nothing more than scribbles and counter-scribbles had transpired, she felt a bubble of excitement rise amid the dread in the pit of her stomach.

The bubble rose. It squeezed through the narrow opening of her esophagus and floated up past her heart, through her chest, into her mouth.

Yes. Go for it! She wanted to shout. Yes. Everything was possible, yes. It was possible.

She should phone her parents. Esther stopped as she reached for the phone. The eyes blinked. Yellow and bloodshot. No. Sofi and Elmar would not want, would not be able, to rejoice. It was too soon. Her family did not believe in magic. Did she? The dread in her stomach gurgled.

NO. No. Estonia could break free if the people wanted to. Esther willed herself to believe it.

She looked down at her watch and was suddenly drawn back into the kitchen by the sound of footsteps coming down, thumping on the bare wood of the stairs. Her hand was shaking. Damn. There wasn't enough time to read the article again, wring every last clue from between the placid grey lines.

She grabbed a magic marker from the jar by the phone and wrote across the top of the paper in blood red: Save This Section For Esther.

◆ K. LINDA KIVI

SOFI ◆ OCTOBER 1944

SHARDS OF GLASS COVER EVERYTHING IN KADRI
Sepp's beautiful apartment like a thick layer of spark-
ling dust. How wonderful, I think, but then catch
myself when I see Kadri's face. Her eyes are huge. She
pulls her breath in quickly, and turns her face away.
What to say? What to do?

Kadri took us in — Helgi, Mamma and me — when
we came to Tallinn with the hospital. We had to move
all the wounded west to Tallinn; the Red Army is
advancing so quickly that if the city walls and
reinforcements didn't stand between us and them,
they'd be here tomorrow. We didn't bother to unpack.

I leave Kadri to go into the living room, stepping
carefully. She follows right behind. Really, there's no

way to be cautious when glass coats every flat surface in her apartment and crunches under the soles of our shoes. It's everywhere except where it's supposed to be. A bomb must have fallen very close by. What if we hadn't had time to hide? I shake the thought out of my head and turn to Kadri.

"So what should we do?" Or should we do anything at all? She doesn't answer.

The late afternoon light pushes in through the open rectangle where the window used to be. The air hangs hazy and thick with the smell of smoke and plaster dust from the bombing. At least this building wasn't hit. Kadri's furniture is more or less intact; the teak coffee table, the fancy couch, the chairs, the embroidered cushions, the dining room furniture, the parquet. Only the sideboard, whose glass windows and display dishes are smashed, is wrecked. But that's where Kadri keeps her treasures. She sees it at the same moment I do.

"Well," I say, more to myself because Kadri doesn't seem to be listening, "I might as well start cleaning." Better to be busy. Better to make the dead, dusty air move.

I take the cushions off the couch, one by one, and shake the glass onto the floor. I get the broom. While I'm sweeping glass off the back of the couch, I notice that there's even glass on the sills of the picture frames above it.

"Look Kadri, even the thatched-roof houses in your paintings lost their windows in the blast." I turn to see her laugh. She doesn't. She is strangely silent.

"Kadri?" I repeat. I hate this quiet and stillness. This feeling that everything has stopped, that our lives have been interrupted. I had plans for today — my only day off from the hospital this week. There will be no one at the Kadriorg park, no civilians, no soldiers. Everyone seems to think that the Soviet planes will be back as soon as they reload.

"So Kadri," I turn to her again, "shouldn't we get some of our things?"

"Yes," she says in a flat monotone, "We don't have long."

"So, what do we take?" She doesn't answer me. "I'll gather Mamma, Helgi and my stuff and you pack what you need. Alright? Kadri?"

She stands in front of the sideboard, looking in at the broken, pretty pieces. With one hand, she reaches in. Her long fingers have perfect nails and her pinkie stretches out as she picks up the fragment of a blue china cup. Kadri has — had — such beautiful things.

"Kadri. No. You'll cut yourself." I go over to her and stand close by without touching. I want her to stop moving so slowly. I want her to be her usual self, laughing and smart, and doing everything just right.

"Oh Sofi," she laments softly, "everything is broken." I don't know what to say. The Kadri I know is the chief nurse in my ward at the hospital; she tells people what to do, how to care for the wounded, what medicines to give and makes those who are dying, or very lonely or sad, smile.

But I don't know how to help this Kadri. All I know is that we need to get some things and go back out to the ice house again. If there's going to be another air raid it's the only safe place.

I leave her standing at the sideboard and crunch into the bedroom. It was Kadri's but she moved onto the couch and gave it up to Mamma, Helgi and I.

I shake glass out of the few things that are sprawled on the bed and dresser — Helgi's warm sweater, the picture book that Emme gave her, Mamma's other panties and brassiere, and my mess — and stuff them in our three suitcases. But how will I carry them without Helgi to help? She stayed behind to watch the children in the shelter, while their mothers went to get their things. She'd be no help here anyway, always dreaming about something instead of working. Or asking about her Mamma.

The hospital kitchen is on the main floor, thank God. I push the first suitcase shut. And the planes can see the hospital's red cross flag during the day, so Mamma should be alright. I close the other suitcases, one after the other, the ones with clasps and the third that we hold together with Isa's leather belt. He got another one with his new uniform. It's been almost seven weeks since he joined the Homeguard and we haven't seen him since. Where is he now? Fighting? Hurt? No. And how will he find us if we move on again?

"Kadri!" I shout from the bedroom, "perhaps we should take the blankets too." No answer. I go see.

Kadri has started moving as though she has woken up. She's swept the glass from a chair and stands on it, near the wall where her blue and gold woolen carpet hangs.

"What are you doing?" I ask.

"I'm taking the carpet down."

"Why?"

"I … We need something to put on the shelter floor. It's cold. Helgi, the children, will catch colds." She takes the top left corner in her hands and yanks hard. It comes loose with a piece of plaster.

"Oh." I can't think of anything to say, but it seems as though there are more important things to take, like food. I wait for her to explain more but she doesn't. She pulls the other corner too. "I'll pack some food," I tell her and head for the kitchen.

Everybody pampers that Helgi, even Kadri. How is she going to grow up, harden a little, if they hold her like a piece of glass?

The cupboards are nearly bare, just half a loaf of bread, some potatoes, a jar of pickles and one with a touch of honey in the bottom, and some grain coffee. Might as well take everything. We can eat the potatoes raw if need be.

"Kadri, how are you going to carry that carpet?" She has cleared the glass from the coffee table and draped the carpet over it.

"Sofi." She anchors my eyes with hers and straightens up. She is tall and thin. When she looks at you with her fine eyebrows arched over those green eyes of hers, you stop and listen. "Help me roll it."

"But what about your things?"

"I'll come back for them next time. In the morning. Besides, nothing really fits anymore."

I hang the bag of food on the door handle and grasp one end of the carpet. I hold the roll closed while Kadri looks for something to tie it with. Through the open bedroom door, I see her squat, awkwardly, to one side and get on her knees to look under the bed. She is usually so easy and elegant.

Of course, it's different now. Though she doesn't say much about it, Kadri is waiting for a baby. And her husband was sent to the front five months ago. If I had a husband, I wouldn't let him go anywhere.

She pulls something out from under the bed and then stands, rubbing the low mound under her loose dress.

"What is it? Is the baby moving?"

"A little. Do you think these will do?" She holds up a pair of cloth belts, one navy, the other brown. The brown one has a pretty brass buckle, probably from one of her outfits. When we first came, she let me try on some of her dresses but the skirts were too long and the bodices tight around my chest so she took them to the hospital for the other girls.

I lift one end of the carpet for Kadri to tie with a belt. Throughout the building, people are talking and shouting now, doors bang, and footsteps echo in the stairwells. She lifts the other end of the carpet and I pull the belt tight and fasten the buckle.

"Kadri, let's look outside?" She nods, and we crunch across the worst of the glass mess to the front window.

"They must have hit the furniture factory down the street again," she says. "I wonder if there was an explosion in there or if this mess is just from the bomb? Good thing they didn't hit the gas station." She laughs her wonderful throaty laugh for the first time since we came into the apartment. It's a laugh that makes the men smile, even if they're hurting. It makes you feel that nothing could be wrong, really.

"What do you think is happening out there?" I say more to myself than anyone in particular and lean out of the jagged hole. Four stories down, the street has come alive again. People scurry across the pitted pavement while one man stops and looks up at us. I wave and just then, the sound of a waltz, someone's gramaphone, rises up from a few floors below.

"Oh, Kadri! There's music." I lean further out to hear better. Is it a waltz? Or something modern? If only there were time to dance.

"Don't fall!" Kadri teases me and takes hold of the back of my dress. "I need you to help move the men. I suspect, after this raid, that we'll be moving the hospital soon. Riga perhaps. Have you ever been to Riga, Sofi?"

"No, but I'd like to go." Has everybody but me been to Riga?

"No? Oh, it's a big city. Bigger than any you've been in. You haven't been to Helsinki, have you? No. Riga will be the biggest one then. It has wonderful stores

— or should I say had. Some people call it the Paris of the Baltic. Who knows what you can get there now. And there were lots of places to dance. I went there on my honeymoon." Kadri strides to the bathroom accompanied by the crunch of glass that is almost becoming normal.

"I can't go anywhere without my lipstick," she shouts from the bathroom.

It's true, she wears a lovely shade of pink that brings out the strawberry highlights in her hair, but she'd be just as beautiful without it. I stand in the bathroom doorway.

"What about me?" I say, and stretch my face towards her. She turns and draws a line on my bottom lip. The lipstick feels wonderfully cool.

"Now rub your lips together. There's a war going on, you know. Rations of lipstick too. Come on. We'd better hurry. It won't be light for long. You take two of the suitcases," she opens the door to the hallway, "and I'll take the third one."

"And the carpet?" I ask.

"Impatient Sofi, wait a second, we'll get to it. You stick one end under your arm and I'll carry the other."

Halfway down the hall I remember the string bag with the food and Kadri goes back for it. When she comes back, I see that she's stuck her husband's picture in the bag, his handsome eyes staring out from between the mesh. We go down four flights of stairs, stumbling and dropping things. Kadri's husband doesn't know about the baby. If we go, how will he find Kadri and his child when he comes home?

Helgi pushes open the ice house door for us and we step into the near dark. I bet there are bugs and worms here. Yuck. When the heavy door swings shut, the blackness swallows us up.

◆ ◆ ◆

When the bombing started yesterday, I didn't have time to get a drink. And when Kadri and I went to get our things after the first raid, I forgot. There was barely any water in the ice house and we gave what we had to the children. After a whole day without any water, I can say this, that a person can live without eating but it's hard to live without drinking.

What to do? I asked some women this morning if they knew where there was water. Nothing. Most of the buildings are flattened and there are enormous holes in the streets. The mains are probably broken. Perhaps, somewhere, there's a spout or someone with a well in their garden, but what if the planes come back? Kadri has gone to the hospital. I can't leave Helgi alone. Not now. All night, a terrible night too — the planes passed again and again, hammering the city with a rain of shells, nobody sleeping, not even me — the children cried and Helgi wouldn't stop asking about Mamma.

"I don't know any more about Mamma than you

do, Helgi," I had to tell her again and again. Until finally, I just told her, "Shut up." She is not used to being scolded and has said nothing since.

When we pushed open the big wooden door this morning, the children grew quiet and Helgi turned white. The first thing we saw was that Kadri's apartment building and the one next to it were gone. Just ruin and rubble. As far as you can see, the neighbourhood is burnt and flattened.

Down the street, the factory walls still stand but the roof has caved in from the fire. There are people everywhere, dragging things out of less damaged buildings. Everything of Kadri's is buried and probably burnt. She went to the hospital right away. At first she wouldn't look at anybody, but when I asked her to find out about Mamma, she turned and put her hand on my shoulder, told me not to worry and smiled.

Where to now? We can't sit here all day picking lint off our coats.

"Helgi, aren't you thirsty?" I ask her as she pokes her thin nose outside.

"Mmmm. *Jah*, a little."

"Why don't we go look for some water? Maybe we can find out what has happened." I can see that she doesn't care.

"But Mamma ..." she answers.

Arrrgh. This girl is too old to be such a baby. Why has Mamma coddled her so? She's not sick anymore. "Helgi," I start, and then pause. There's no point in getting angry with her, she'll just snail into her shell further. I try again. "Helgi, Mamma is probably helping with the new wounded at the hospital. We'll go to the hospital when we find water. Okay?"

She looks doubtful. "But the tram lines are broken."

"Then we'll walk," I raise my voice and turn away.

"I'll come with you, Sofi." Helgi stands up, pushes her skirt down. It barely covers her knobbly knees. Where we'll get her another, I don't know.

We walk toward town, through the middle of the street. Cars are few; rubble fills the street and we have to climb over mound after mound. Tatar Street takes us toward town.

Everywhere there are people. Most of them run busily from one ruined place to another but some, like the woman with the snowball bun at her nape who we ask for directions to water, just sit on the curb. She rocks a little.

"Please. Do you know where there's water?" I ask.

"The angels will come help our boys," the woman's voice shakes and I don't understand what she's talking about. I must look puzzled because she repeats herself, looking right past Helgi and me, "the angels will come help our boys, like they did before."

The woman is crazy. "Where do you live?" I ask, maybe we can help her home or find someone that knows her.

"Yes. They came up out of the snow, the angels did," she answers and then keeps going. "And when the Russian soldiers saw that we had God's warriors on our side, they ran away, afraid. They dropped their guns and didn't stop to pick up their watercans. They just ran until their boots split and fell and their foot rags unravelled. Our men thought that they had beaten them with their might. But no. My husband saw. He was lying on his back in the snow, a bullet in his shoulder bone, and he saw the angels rise up, their wings as wide as clouds."

"Where is your husband now?" She looks at me blankly. "Where are your children?" I try.

"Hundreds of them. There were hundreds of angels, he said."

Her voice is almost ecstatic. She can't help us and I don't know how to help her. I turn away and take Helgi by the sleeve so that she won't stay and listen. We walk toward the old city again.

As we go, I can still hear her talking. Crazy, poor woman. "They won the war for us. God is on our side. He will chase the Russians away again."

Everywhere, I ask about water. I ask a man with a red nose and grey felt hat. I ask a woman with a little boy in short pants who answers back in Russian. My thirst becomes more and more fierce, until my throat is so dry that it hurts to talk.

Nobody knows about the water. Some point us this way, others another. We keep going, Helgi tagging behind me like a tail that's forgotten how to wag.

Finally, I see a woman coming down the hill from where the government buildings are with a pail. From the way it swings as she walks, I can tell its empty. I watch where she goes and we follow her. She turns into a small side street. Saliva runs in my mouth. There's water there. There has to be.

The street is narrow and winds through the outer perimeter of the old city. The streets are cobblestone and hard to balance on with my heeled shoes. Helgi's are flat, but they're ugly, too. Sure enough, there's water running in the street, over the cobblestones. The woman, a good-looking, well-dressed, older woman, fills her bucket at a spout. I realize then that we don't have anything to carry water with.

The woman at the spout looks up at me. She has kind eyes. "We just need to drink," I say, and she moves her bucket so that I can cup my hands under the spout. Oooh. Relief.

She looks at me, then at Helgi who hangs back, shy. "What's happened?"

"Everything has happened, and we haven't had anything to drink since yesterday. Kadri's apartment block is gone."

"Oi! And you probably haven't had anything to eat either," she says.

"That doesn't matter so much. It's just that I've been horribly thirsty."

"This water is dreadfully cold. It'll hurt your stomach. Come up to my apartment and I'll make you a cup of coffee. I don't have the real thing but I've got grain coffee and I'll give you a piece of bread too."

"Oh, no. You don't need to ..." I start to say but she interrupts quietly.

"Come."

Helgi and I carry the pail, grasping the metal handle from either side. We carry it up to Toompea, on the hill above the old town, very careful not to lose a single drop over the edges. We arrive at a thin yellow house and step inside. The stairs seem very old and mysterious.

Inside her apartment, the walls are dotted with paintings and her windows are whole.

She gives us each a small piece of black bread. "I'm sorry I don't have anything to put on it."

It doesn't matter. I am only glad that her house has not been hurt. There are vases and statues, one of a man's head in bronze, and lamps with fringes around the bottom. Helgi sits on a dark red velvet couch and starts to eat the dry bread. I can't sit. I can't eat yet. My mouth is too dry.

The woman brings our coffee. *Äiteh.* I nudge Helgi to thank her too. This is a place to remember your manners. The coffee is not too hot and so, so good.

◆ K. LINDA KIVI

◆ WINTER 1989

THE LAB WAS DARK EXCEPT FOR THE PATCH OF flourescent blue light that surrounded the work table. Absentmindedly, Esther poured the last of the warm agar into a white enamel tray; it would gel overnight. Tomorrow they would slice the gels and run them to see, in time, what patterns the purple spots would reveal on the smooth surface. Though Esther's prof — now her employer — was ensconced in the complexities of his genetic research, the actual work of preparing the gels was more or less rote: measure, blend, pour, and set the trays in the refrigerators that stood like a line of soldiers against the back wall of the lab.

The lab gave Esther the spooks sometimes, especially

when she was working late, by herself. The basement of the botany building was forever dim and the ceiling hung low with interlaced pipes and tubes of all dimensions. The pipes seemed to carry voices from the floors above. Esther would sometimes spin around to see who was behind her only to discover that she was alone in the lab. People rarely came down to visit. Esther usually didn't mind this. It gave her time to be with her own thoughts.

She had taken to designing houses in her head as she worked. Her latest version — not yet copied down into the unlined book she kept in the top drawer of her desk at home — had windows on all sides of its one cavernous room. Tall, clear windows, she imagined, that left nothing obscured, nothing hidden, and invited in the sloping winter sunshine.

It was hard to design a house and gardens, Esther realized, without having a clue as to where they would be planted — among a stand of level poplars, perched on a steep hillside or gripping the rocks at a river's edge? Where indeed? A house with no earth under it was no house at all.

Esther set the last tray down and gazed at the palms of her hands. They were waxen and pasty from lab work. She turned them over. At least when she was doing her own research, planting endless replicates of her peas in soil innoculated with different strains of mycorrhizal fungi, her nails were dark with encrusted soil. She had to rub cream into them nightly to keep them moist. Working hands. That's what she admired. Like Vanaema's short heavy fingers or Elmar's muscled palms and wrists.

Esther was the only one in her family that had made it past high school. And although Sofi and Elmar had wanted — no, expected — her to go to university, they were baffled by her decision to study agriculture. The New World promised so much; anyone could become a doctor, a lawyer, a biochemist, professions which offered security, respect and cleanliness. Esther suspected that Elmar, the gardener, was secretly pleased with his youngest daughter's desire to unearth the secrets of plants, but he did not dare contradict Sofi.

"And what kind of husband are you going to find there?" she had raged, slamming lids onto bubbling pots on the stove. "A farmer." The last shreds of Esther's indecision over what to study burnt away in the disdain of Sofi's voice. Later, she wondered if she had stayed with agriculture and gone on to do her Masters just to defy Sofi and claim her own ground in the process.

Her own ground. Hmmm. Had her decision been that literal? Though she had excelled in biology at high school, sketching perfect colour-coded diagrams of the functions of a leaf with gusto, it was a reoccuring image of herself that inspired Esther's choice of career. In a lumber jacket and a sunny straw hat, she stood in a green tree-ringed field, the furrows uneven beneath her gumboots, a sagging farmhouse squatting at the end of a gravel lane beyond a line of wooden fence. The first few months at university had been a disappointment; her rubber boots had glumly kept vigil on the mud mat by the front door, occasionally damp but never dirty. In time, in time, she would mutter to her boots as she hugged her fat textbooks to her chest and headed for school.

Then, when Esther decided to keep on with school instead of finding a "good job" with the Ministry of Agriculture or a research firm, Sofi had simply turned her back in exasperation. What could she do with two degrees in agriculture? What purpose did all this studying have? Yes, her parents had wanted her to reach for what they could not have, but not what they didn't want. Esther's aspirations had grown beyond their grasp and the world of academia had taken her as one of their own. And now she had betrayed their hopes too. The right thing from their perspective was a Pea Aitch Dee. To what end? To join the shrinking world of people who knew so much about such little things? When she had started her second degree, she had rebelled, wanting to study how things interconnected, not how they came apart. But she had found little support among the faculty or her peers.

Serious research involved intricacies. It involved identifying with one plant, one animal, or one pest exclusively. Esther liked her research with peas because the system with the mycorrhiza that mingled among their roots fascinated her. Over the past two years, her cohorts had supplied her with a collection of pea paraphernalia: t-shirts, cartoons, even a stuffed plush pea pod with detachable peas stuck on with velcro.

At the last horticultural conference, there had been a vegetable clothing contest and the guy with the bicycling gear, a hollowed out half pumpkin for a helmet and zucchinis and eggplants strapped to his elbows and knees for pads, had won.

School did this to people. Made them hilarious. Pushed the edges of sense back while trying to inspire nothing but good sense and logic. They had it all wrong, Esther often thought. Being a grad student was a little like joining a cult. Deprived of sleep and social contact outside a milieu of like-minded obsessives, the world had a tendency to flatten out and become as small as it was big.

Esther carried the last of the trays to the refrigerators. The large, numbered clock on the wall gave its odd hourly groan as the big hand strained into place. Seven o'clock. Brenda was late. The lecture would be starting. Damn. Why did she agree to go? Esther shrugged her winter jacket on. Home sounded good after a long day of blending, pouring and then watching to see whether the gels would do their thing.

Esther had only heard of bioregionalism and permaculture in passing and knew that her colleagues greeted the posters for the lecture with scorn. "Pseudoscience!" one of her labmates had snorted. According to the poster, it was an "integrated and sustainable approach to agriculture and living" that had been developed in Australia. Esther was interested in seeing where these so-called pseudo-scientific notions fit in with her own. She was curious about what kind of people went to these lectures.

More snow was falling when she reached the doors of the Botany building. For once, it wafted down vertically instead of slicing sideways propelled by the fierce wind. February had been especially bitter. It was almost over, she reminded herself daily. In only two months, pea planting season — when the earth would be bare and damp, crocuses nosing up from among last year's dead grass — would be at hand. Maybe she'd know what she was doing with her life by then.

Brenda, bundled like the Michelin man in her white parka, rounded the corner of the building. Esther put her shoulder to the heavy glass door and joined her housemate half way down the path. Without the wind, the cold kissed her skin instead of biting, asked to enter gently instead of tearing at the flaps of her jacket. Esther wished for a moment that she could just lie in the snow and sleep, but Brenda had already taken her arm, was telling her about her day.

Later, after the lecture, Esther felt the same urge to lie down, only this time, she'd make snow angels instead of curling up in the drifts. She put her cool hands against her hot cheeks. A warm humming filled Esther's chest.

She rocked from foot to foot on the snowy steps as she and Brenda waited for their ride home. How could you help but like a woman who begins her talk with a poem of Ursula K. LeGuin's about northern B.C.? Esther was familiar with her novels but didn't know she wrote poetry. How did it go? *Land forms / the mind. / Ideas fill these bogs.* She couldn't remember the rest. Louise — the speaker — had recited the words by heart, without looking down at her notes, her bright eyes dark and shining.

There was something about Louise's enthusiasm, her wide-sweeping vision, her belief that it was possible to build homes, lives and communities that could exist in mutual respect, that struck Esther. And she knew her material.

The agricultural concepts that Louise presented were well-grounded and well-researched, even though Esther knew that her colleagues would find some of them a little unrealistic. Esther had been the first to ask a question when Louise concluded her talk.

"In your model, is it possible to grow crops, grain for example, without pesticides, and still meet the market needs of this country?" The question had come out harsher than Esther intended. It sounded like a challenge.

If Louise perceived the tone of challenge, she did not respond to it. She talked about bioregionalism not as a way of maintaining the current economy, which was run by the banks, but as an alternative system. "It isn't a question of reform, it's a question of total, fundamental change in the way we supply ourselves with food and shelter and community."

Esther's hand had shot up again. "And is it practiced anywhere, really? And on what scale?"

Esther wiped the snowflakes off her eyelashes. No,

even if some people built solar houses and fertilized their gardens with manure from the chicken coop, bioregionalism was positively utopian. It would never work. And yet, Esther could not still the spinning in her chest and the image of Louise's vivid eyes whenever she mentioned her home, a place where Louise obviously felt she belonged. Esther felt inspired by and afraid for Louise at the same time. It didn't pay to be that enthusiastic. Optimism and happiness made people greedy for your demise.

When the question period ended and the cluster of thirty-odd people — most of them artsy students wearing Peruvian sweaters and funny hats — filed out of the hall, Esther had followed mutely, knowing there was something more she needed to know. She had fired question after question at Louise, and Louise had answered them all without hesitation. What was it that she had failed to ask?

Esther turned to Brenda. "I forgot something. Wait, okay? I won't be a minute." She took the steps two at a time.

When she pushed open the door to the lecture hall, Louise was talking to a few eager students who had stayed behind. Esther hesitated. They all seemed so bright-eyed and young. Louise turned and caught her eye, smiled and gestured for Esther to come over. Without a word, Louise jotted something down on a piece of paper that she reached out to Esther.

"A resource list," she said, when the other students evaporated. "I thought you might come back. You seem keen on considering what I'm talking about."

"I'm an agriculture student," Esther answered though she knew that that wasn't what Louise meant. Her questions hadn't been about permaculture at all, they'd been about feasability, vision, and society's consumer orientation. They had come from the part of Esther that was afraid to want what she dreamt of.

Louise gazed at Esther steadily, her dark curls framing her questioning expression.

Esther continued, "I'm actually done now. I've been trying to figure out what to do next. Thinking of leaving Winnipeg. Seeing what people are doing elsewhere." Esther startled herself with this revelation, to a total stranger too.

"I thought you might be interested in seeing how we practice what we preach," Louise said, gesturing at the paper in Esther's hand.

Esther looked down at her boots. "Yeah," she muttered, turning to go, "I … Thanks for the talk."

As she stepped out into the hallway she glanced at the sheet Louise had given her. At the top, written in a sprawling hand, was an address in British Columbia. Louise's address. A rural address. This is what Esther had wanted to know: where to find others who had similar dreams.

Esther folded the paper into a thick wad and stuffed it into the front pocket of her jeans. Why not go?

For once, the voice in her head that usually answered with a million reasons why not, paused for a second before it began its rant.

HELGI ◆ NOVEMBER 1944

MAMMA WAS WRINGING HER HANDS WHEN THE letter from Isa came. Somebody brought it to the hospital where we are in Leibau, in Latvia, from a ship. Sofi says if we're lucky, this ship will take us out of here. I've never been on a ship before. I've never been in a bag before either.

The soldier with the bandage around his head who whimpers in his sleep says we're in a bag. My job is to wake him if he has a bad dream; he asked me to. I also take the bed pans away.

I try to imagine a bag the size of this city, a sack big enough to hold all the stone buildings, all the army trucks and trains, all the people. But I know from the faces of everybody in the hospital, on the street, that it's true. We are in trouble. The Russians have surrounded us. But what will they do if we cannot keep them out? Nobody wants to answer my question. They all say that we won't be here when it happens. There's a ship coming to take us away, maybe the same one that Isa's letter came on.

Isa would answer my questions if he were here. Emme would tell me something too. I miss her. She wanted me to take the blue blanket with me but Mamma said we couldn't carry it. Too big. Too heavy. And my arms are too skinny. Even Kadri says so.

We are going to Germany. Where Isa is. In a boat so big that it doesn't have oars or even a sail. Maybe he'll be waiting for us there. Maybe we'll all have a house together again. Maybe we'll have a cat.

Where is Nurr? Winter is coming. Mamma lets me read Isa's letter by myself. *Kallis Mari, Sofi ja Helgi,* he starts. Me at the end because I'm the youngest.

I have arrived in Germany. Where will this letter find you? I'm sending it through the Feldpost, to your hospital in Tallinn, even though I hope you have already left. The Red Army is moving so quickly that the Germans can barely take their artillery and wounded with them. The last I heard, the Russian lines could be seen from the towers of old Tallinn. I hope that the hospital has been able to take care of you. You must evacuate with them, whereever they go. Your best chance is to stay with them. And to stay together — all three of you. Sofi too.

What else could we do if not stay together?

Sofi: this is not the time to go galavanting on your

own. Listen to Mamma and help take care of Helgi. Please.

The soldiers in your hospital will be sent to Germany and dispersed to hospitals, wherever there is space. Try to get a posting to Southern Germany. People here in Danzig say that it will be safest away from Berlin if the Russians march all the way to Germany. Maybe the Allied forces will be there to meet them and hold them back. Maybe not. You know who you need to run from as well as I do.

Yes. The Red Army. Those men who stood around the train station and the cafeteria in Narva, smoking cigarettes, laughing and making the girls blush as they walked past. They never said anything to me. The German soldiers are the same except that they've begun to notice me too. They always say things in German and Sofi won't tell me what, so I don't know. Sofi sometimes gets mad at the boys in the hospital but I can tell she likes it too. Mamma says that she should stay away from them. Isa thinks so too, but he's not here to tell her again and again like he used to in Rakvere.

As I write this, I am at the SS transit camp in Danzig. The German boats in Kuresaare were taking anyone in uniform, even the Homeguard. They couldn't get off the island fast enough. The Soviet navy was shelling boats that had not even left the harbour. The island people filled their fishing boats and fled to Sweden in the night. It is said that both the Russians and the Germans try to shoot at them and no one knows how many get through. My own ship was hit when it was still in the bay and we all jumped into the drink. One boy from my unit could not swim but we managed, with one other man, to pull him to shore.

Who will pull me to shore if our boat sinks into the sea? Mamma never let me swim when the others did. She said it would hurt my lungs. My lungs hurt even without swimming, from all the coughing and sputtering that the sickness caused. I didn't want to go in anyway. The Baltic is cold, even in August.

The boy's fingers were as blue as the night. Mine less so because I kept moving. There were six from my unit with me on the boat that finally sailed without mishap. Others — mostly younger ones — went into the forests and bogs, to fight from there. I thought to go too, but I have you to think of and find a home for.

Home? Where? At least until the war is over and we can go back. We'll have to dig up the pots, pans and the cutlery. Only I know where the ladle is. And Mamma's begonias will be wanting water and the lilac bushes that she and Isa planted when I came home from the sanatorium last time will bloom in the spring. But will Nurr still be there?

From this transit camp in Danzig, we are being sent to a place near Berlin — here is the address. From there, I'll try to get out of uniform and go south too — to Bavaria. They want to press everyone into German uniform but I'm too old for this. And they must know that we won't fight against the Allies, only the Russians, but they are becoming so desperate that even an old man like me is not safe. I love you all very much and we'll be together again soon. I promise.

He signs his name — *Juhan* — like Mamma calls him, not Isa. Emme's neighbour had a son called Juhan. Juhan had a dog named Muri. Muri was black, with big round yellow eyes. Our ship will go to Germany in the dark.

◆ SPRING 1989

WHEN VANAEMA SQUATTED, SHE LOOKED LIKE AN egg, back rounded against the pull of her plain brown dress, as if laid by some large bird in the even deeper brown of the upturned soil. Esther leaned her weight against the spade, caught her breath and let the singing in her back muscles quiet. She had spent the morning digging, spooning the earth to one side so that she could loosen the soil below. Vanaema's earth was heavy. And chocolaty rich. She had been carrying out honey buckets laden with kitchen scraps as long as Esther could remember, long before it became popular to compost. Elmar had replaced her original bins twice already, the design evolving so that the two slatted boxes in the back corner of the small yard looked just like his.

Every spring, Esther laid the dank organic matter, flecked white with shattered egg shells, onto the garden before she turned the soil. Vanaema would plant in the wake of her work.

Esther watched her grandmother as she shook a handful of carrot seeds from a paper packet into her pink palm. With the side of her other hand, she made a furrow, to match the one on her concentrated brow, and sprinkled the minute seeds in a long even line. She laid out the next row in just the same way, her plump, liver-spotted hands moving in a familiar dance across the earth. One, two, three, pat down the soil. One, two …

Esther picked up the watering can. Vanaema liked to water the newly covered grains every half bed. Esther dipped the can into the rain barrel that gathered what the roof of the little green house collected. "Seeds, like people," Vanaema often told Esther, "need warm water in their bellies. The cold just makes us shrivel up."

Vanaema had always had lots to say about *Pakane*, the frost or cold, a personage that kept a greedy eye on children. When Esther had wanted to sit on the front step and watch the world spin, it was Vanaema, not Sofi, who ran interference.

"Pakane will chill your bladder. Don't sit on bare cement!" And when it was a bomber jacket that she wanted to buy, later, when looking like her friends mattered, Vanaema forbade it. "Your kidneys will catch cold," she insisted though Esther had never heard of such a thing. In spite of all Pakane's intrigues, Vanaema only wore a kerchief over her thin hair, knotted loosely at her throat, even when the winter winds howled through the streets of January.

She had come out without her kerchief on this warm spring morning. And Esther had bared her white thighs for the first time this year. Her shorts were a bit tight, she noted, winter's layer still thick on her solid hips. It was good to be in the garden again. This was Esther's favourite time of year. And the garden was her favourite place.

Esther turned to see Vanaema raise a pinch of soil to her mouth. She held it against her barely parted lips and, in the blink of an eye that later Esther would not be able to remember nor forget, the earth was gone and the old woman had laid another indentation in the garden.

Water slopped on Esther's legs as she carried the can to the most recently planted bed. Vanaema couldn't lift it anymore. Esther watched the thin arcs of water catch the sunlight as they fell. She sprinkled the last of Vanaema's work and then helped the egg that was her grandmother stand up.

Helgi would be home with the groceries soon. "Time to make lunch," she said, pointing to her bare wrist. Sometimes Vanaema didn't hear anymore. It was as if she was spending time in a place that had a thick sponge of years for walls and she would forget where the door was. Vanaema looped her arm through

Esther's crooked elbow and together they made their way over the uneven grass to the back door. Esther helped her up the two low stairs.

"Äiteh Leoni," she said as the wooden screen door clapped shut behind them.

Leoni? Why did Vanaema call her Leoni? The name was somehow familiar yet Esther couldn't place it.

Vanaema reached a pot of borscht out of the fridge and Esther turned on the stove. The ring of blue flame leapt to attention and the condensation on the bottom of the pot sizzled as it burned away. Esther scrubbed her hands under the warm stream from the tap.

"Helgi will bring fresh sour cream and bread," Vanaema mumbled, more to herself than Esther, as she lowered herself onto a white wooden kitchen chair. Esther pulled out the one opposite and took her grandmother's hand to catch her attention.

"Vanaema," she patted the warm hand, *"Kes on Leoni?"*

"Leoni." Vanaema's face relaxed into an odd youthfulness, the furrow falling from her brow as she repeated the name. "He is my brother. My twin."

Esther could barely stay in her seat. What? "I didn't know you had a twin, a brother ..." she ventured, confused, trying not to let on about her concern. Was Vanaema loosing it completely? "Where is he?"

"At home," she answered so simply that Esther knew that it was true. Without prompting, she added, "at home in Russia."

"You mean Estonia? Right?" Something was

definitely amiss here.

"Oh no," Vanaema shook her head sadly, "my father took only me in the boat. The soldiers had already taken Leoni." She dipped her head then and a strand of her fine mousey hair fell forward over her nose. Esther saw that her hand shook lightly when she reached to tuck it behind her ear again. When she looked up at her granddaughter, there was a grain of water in her eye. "He used to put the worm on the hook for me. And he would give me his pencil to use at school when mine broke. He was more careful than me."

Esther could see that Vanaema had disappeared into the sponge room again. She wished she could follow. Unravel this strangeness. How did an Estonian grandmother suddenly have a twin brother named Leoni in Russia? Esther rose and took out the long wooden spoon. The soup swirled magenta and left orange droplets of fat against the sides of the white enamel pot. It swirled faster and faster as she pushed the wooden spoon around the sides of the pot bumping into chunks of potato and cabbage, and leaving a deep hole in the centre.

The fierce barking of the neighbour's yellow-eyed mongrel stopped Esther's spoon. Helgi was home. What did Helgi know?

Six paper bags of groceries lined the backseat of the Buick like well behaved children. Esther leaned against the house to admire them and caught the thread of a klezmer tune that wafted down the street, the clarinet line snaking between the houses. She picked up the first two bags and carried them inside, her thoughts twisting and spiraling like the music, a tune too fast to catch hold of.

Esther carried in the last two bags, and emptied their contents onto the counter: brown paper-wrapped lengths of sausage, jars and cans and bags of fruit. Helgi stood on a chair, shifting cans, piling them high on a shelf in an attempt to stuff even more into the already overflowing cupboards. The refrigerator was just as full. Helgi would have to put the groceries away herself. At both Helgi and Sofi's houses, there was no such thing as too much food, as if anything less than a year's supply was cause for distress.

When Helgi was done, they sat down to lunch and Helgi told her mother about everyone she had seen in her morning travels — about the other old women who still went to the Polish delicatessen where they had shopped for years, every Saturday morning. They did not seem to notice that Esther's attention was elsewhere.

It was too strange; to be versed — no, coached — in one version of history only to discover, at such a late date, that it was a half truth. And yet, what difference should it make, a few kilometres with a line called a border in between? But that wasn't the point. Esther felt cheated. Shortchanged. If Vanaema was Russian, then who was this almost forgotten man who rowed aside the night to take his daughter to what he hoped was safety? And who was it that kept

Vanaema quiet all these years?

It wasn't until Esther was laying the dishes into the sink that she finally found words to open her pit of questions.

"Helgi, who is Leoni?" Helgi turned toward Esther, eyes as wide as a deer caught in the headlights, and then turned away again, twisting the taps on full. The sink nearly overflowed with suds before she spoke.

"Who told you?" she finally asked.

"Vanaema, of course," Esther stumbled. Who told her wasn't the point at all. She wanted to know the story. "Why the secret? I don't understand." A sudden tinge of anger burned at Esther's temples. "Why have you lied to me all these years, about Vanaema being from Estonia?"

Helgi sighed. She was never good at confrontation. She gathered up her breath and began, "We lied because that was what Mamma and Isa wanted. During the war. Mamma had a false passport — an Estonian one that said she was born in Estonia — because she had come secretly. Illegally. Then, the war. It wasn't safe. We knew that they would take her, and maybe us — Sofi and me, not Isa, he was Estonian through and through — if they found out. It just stayed that way." She stopped and looked at Esther. "Besides, you know how Estonians are."

Esther did. Russians were scum to Estonians, even among her generation of kids who had never suffered at the hands of the Soviets themselves. How would her Toronto friends have looked upon her if they knew she was part Russian? The lurch of her stomach startled her. This hatred was bred into them, sucked in with their mother's milk and every mouthful since. And suddenly, to find that the so-called enemy's blood coursed in her own veins. She didn't know what to think.

"But Vanaema's Estonian is so good."

"She was only 17 when she slipped over the border. And she hasn't seen her family since." Helgi paused, and smiled quietly, "but I think she's started to visit with them again. In her mind. She's missed them. Leoni especially."

Esther picked up one of the old and worn dishes that Vanaema never wanted to replace, and wiped it slowly. The silence seemed to reduce their gestures to slow motion, as if they were making their way through a thick and sticky fog.

It was Helgi who spoke at last. "Does this change anything for you?"

"I don't know. We're still who we are. I just don't understand how you, of all people, didn't tell me the truth."

Helgi pulled her niece toward her and wrapped her thin arms around her. It was so rare to be touched by Helgi, Helgi who took after her father who was long gone, the Estonian one, the cool one. She melted into her aunt's tentative hug. When she let go, Esther realized that the reason her family touched and hugged each other more than other Estonians was probably because Vanaema was Russian. It was more their way.

Esther looped the tea towel through the fridge handle and went to find Vanaema. She sat in her chair by the front window; Esther took the brush down from the bookshelf and plunked down on the floor at her feet. Vanaema patted Esther's hair and began to brush, lifting up the layers of light brown curls and letting them fall as she pulled the brush through.

Esther took a deep breath. Would Vanaema tell her more? "So why did the soldiers take Leoni and not you?"

"Because I was the girl." Vanaema didn't hesitate. "We were both in the same political group. It turned out not to be the right one even though we wanted many of the same things that the Bolsheviks did. What we wanted most, was land for everybody. Yes," she nodded as if to agree with herself, "that was what we wanted. Land enough for everyone to feed themselves."

The brush pulled harder and Vanaema continued, with more words than Esther had heard from her in a long time. Suddenly, it had become okay to remember, to be who she was, from the beginning, not just from some windy night when a darkened sea parted the pieces of now and then forever. "I even said things at the meetings," she continued. "Leoni was the quiet one. After my father took me to Estonia, I became both, the quiet one and the one who talked. That was how I knew they killed him."

She paused. "It's hard to be a twin. But it's harder without him. You must keep an eye on Kadri's boys.

You watch over them. Always."

It was a command that demanded a commitment. "*Jah Vanaema. Jah.*"

Esther looked up. Helgi was leaning on the doorframe, watching, her lips parted as if there were something else she wanted to say, her eyes bright and sad all at once.

"Come." Esther patted the other armchair, the blue one, Helgi's chair. Helgi sunk quietly into her chair and folded one long leg over the other. Esther followed her gaze out the window into the street.

The neighbourhood children chased a soccer ball up and down the street, squealing with the warmth of the first spring sunshine on their pale skins. Helgi and Vanaema knew them all, for at least a block. They would often come, in ones or twos, later in the afternoon when they were tired of racing about and hurried, testy mothers sent them back out until dinner was ready. Vanaema and Helgi always had apple juice on hand though neither of them drank it. Or if a knee was scraped or a child rebuffed by the gang, there were slices of Ryvita slathered with butter and honey. And though the ones that Esther had played with when she was little had grown up and moved away, they came to visit her aunt and grandmother when they were in the neighbourhood.

Esther had often wondered, as an adult, whether Helgi wouldn't have wanted children of her own, but she never dared to ask. Helgi hadn't even married. Would things have been different if the war hadn't torn their lives apart? Would Helgi have found a gentle Estonian farm boy and raised pigs and chickens, vegetables and a child? What did the people who stayed behind do with their lives? Who would she, Esther, be if things had gone differently. What did women her age dream about in Estonia?

Esther looked up at Helgi to catch Helgi looking at her. Her aunt rubbed her chin and opened her mouth twice before she finally spoke. "You're thinking of going to Estonia," she said, a statement not a question. It was uncanny how Helgi always knew these things, and with such certainty.

Esther shook her head and smiled. She had told no one about the visa forms that had come from the Soviet embassy, to be filled out in triplicate.

"Can I come with you?" Helgi asked.

What? Esther looked intently at her aunt. Was she serious? Helgi, who would never speak about the homeland. Helgi, who never argued with Sofi and Elmar when they criticized their friends who had chosen to visit Estonia in the past few years: "They're just supporting the Soviets; we won't go until Estonia is completely free." Helgi, who hadn't travelled any further than Lake Winnipeg in forty years.

"Of course ... I don't see why not. Yes. Come with me," Esther stammered. But did Helgi really mean it? Wasn't she afraid, given what Esther now knew? Helgi was not just a Soviet citizen by their estimation, but certainly a Russian citizen to boot. Esther still remembered when the Soviets had passed the law that made anyone who was born on Soviet soil, and their offspring, Soviet citizens. And even from the safety of their Winnipeg homes, they had laughed warily. The law only confirmed what her parents and their friends already knew in their hearts: the Communists wanted them, every last one of them.

Helgi read her thoughts again, or maybe they were her own, because she sounded as though she were reassuring herself. "It'll be okay. My passport is in order. What would they do with an old woman like me?"

"And everything seems quiet at the moment," she added. It had amazed them all. After the bid for sovereignty, nothing serious had transpired. The Soviets passed a series of countermotions and laws, but no soldiers had marched on the tiny Republic, no tanks had rolled. And all of the Baltic states, not just Estonia, were stretching their Soviet-digested limbs towards the newly, if only partially, independent sky. There was talk of an independent currency — the kroon. There was talk of redistributing land from the collective and state farms back to their pre-war owners.

But Esther needed to see it in order to believe it. What would they find there? Would she know anything, anybody? Or was it all so changed, that her parents' fairy tales had become just that? Where would they go, where would they stay? And …

"And Vanaema?" Esther asked out loud, looking up to see that her grandmother's eyes, pale disks, were vacant and distant.

"She won't be coming with us. I've already asked Kadri, that if I needed to go anywhere, would she come and stay with Mamma."

"And?"

"She said yes. That Bob could look after the twins."

"For a change," Esther added.

"That's what she said," Helgi looked at Esther with surprise. Sometimes, Helgi was as unperceptive as she was in tune. How could she know so much and so little at the same time? To be able to look into Esther's dreams but not see that Kadri's marriage was in trouble?

MARIA ◆ NOVEMBER 1944

THE LONG, HIGH WHISTLE IS FOR US. FOR US. THE torpedo whines through the Baltic night waters, an arrow in search of a heart. The darkness thickens. We are as quiet as mice in the belly of this iron whale.

The ship's engine throbs with the same rhythm as my aching tooth. Both throb and throb. My ears are full of this terrible quiet.

Then comes the whistling. A torpedo. Growing closer, the whistling grows into a whine. Sounds of life and sounds of death. I hold Helgi tight against my chest. Sofi grasps my hand. Oh God who made us all and Mary, mother of Jesus, spare us our tiny lives Oh God who made us all and Mary, mother of Jesus, spare us ... Silence and darkness grip. I pray silently, like I have for years. I call on Juhan. I call on Leoni. I press my heel against the gold ruble in my shoe. I call on the Virgin mother. We wait long years as the whine grows louder. It is throbbing too as it spins through the water toward us.

Louder still. Oh God!

Missed.

The room breathes again but no one speaks. The captain asked everyone to be quiet until we pass the Russian base on shore. The ship turned out its lights. And we, ten women, the only ones on this ship of wounded men, need to keep the lights inside alive. Always one step ahead of the Red Army. Only one step ahead ...

They nearly caught our train leaving Tallinn. They nearly bagged us when they surrounded Leibau. And now? How lucky will we be again? Will any of us see sunrise in Danzig? At least Juhan is already there. So many have failed the test of the Baltic.

"Mamma," Sofi whispers.

"Ssssshh."

"I want to go to the ward, where Kadri is."

"No. That was only the first. Quiet now. Stay with us."

Sofi cannot get enough of Kadri, that beautiful, beautiful Kadri wanting to fix everybody's life but her own. That baby in her belly will be here sooner than she thinks.

The whistle. Again. So soon. I rub my swollen cheek. The Red Army wants us to swim. All movement stills.

All movement stills except the neverending throb of the engine, the heart that beats, the lung that breathes while we hold ourselves as silent as death.

The whistle grows.
And the whistle grows.

Missed.

We wait for the next one. And pray.

◆ K. LINDA KIVI

◆ SUMMER 1989

THE SQUAT GREEN MOSKVITS, THE STANDARD
budget Soviet car, roared as if to lend itself courage as
it bumped over the rutted road. It was hard to believe
that this was the main highway that linked Tallinn to
Leningrad. After Esther, Helgi and the driver had
driven a few hours out of Tallinn, the road had begun
to erode. In fact, the whole country seemed imbued
with a pernicious form of decay that started with the
buildings and moved inward, into people's hearts.
There was no end to the stories of Soviet injustices,
about men rounded up for the Chernobyl cleanup
who were now perishing from cancer, of women ar-
rested for hemming neighbours' dresses, of the disappeared. Even her cousins' laughter was acrid.

It was a relief to sit quietly. Esther's eardrums stung at the end of each day. She had begun to look forward to bedtime, when she could lay her head, full and throbbing, on the cool linen of a pillow. Each one of her many relatives had a story to tell, a joke about the inefficencies and stupidities of the Soviet system, and a barrage of questions about The West. It wasn't that she didn't want to hear and answer. No. It was just that there was too much, a red river of venom that seemed to have no end.

Only Elmar's cousin Liisi seemed to understand that she and Helgi wanted other things as well. The forest. The seashore. To visit Emme's grave and the house that Helgi had lived in with her grandmother during the war. The little house where Helgi was born. Places that once were home.

Esther pressed her cheek against the cool window and looked up into the sky. The expanse of blue and white was much the same as it had been the day she and Helgi sailed from Helsinki; the low sheepy puffs moved so quickly it was as if there was a fox in their midst. Nobody had told her about the sky. She had not known it would be so different, so close.

Much had been that way — unexpected and beautiful — layered between the things she had been taught that she would find. You can know about a bog and the red berries that your ancestors picked there without knowing what it is to have your footsteps spring back beneath you in the thick pungent moss. It was Liisi who had taken them to a spot by the lake where they gathered lingonberries. And it was Liisi and Helgi who had hauled Esther out of the ditch that had looked like solid ground until Esther put her foot down and sank hip-deep into the green muck.

Esther was glad that she had come to see for herself. To hear for herself.

A small flock of enormous black and white magpies circled and screeched over a field beside the road. Beyond them, in the distance, Esther noticed the rise of smooth pale hills, perfectly conical, too perfect to be natural. She leaned across the front seat and shouted to the driver.

"What are those hills?"

"Ash," he answered and Esther thought she hadn't heard right. She asked again and he repeated himself. "Ash. From the tar sands production." He didn't explain further but Esther knew. These were the hills that made children's hair fall out and poisoned the ground water for miles. She leaned forward again.

"This must be the area where the proposed phosphate mines are too." The driver only grunted in response.

It was strange to find herself among a whole country of people who spoke in the secret tongue of her childhood yet were strangers and did not pretend otherwise. In Canada, every Estonian was practically family. Here, Esther and Helgi were novelties, guests, even among Elmar's relatives. They were relegated to the dark living room when the others went to peel potatoes or milk the cows. They were offered everything, anything that was there to be offered. Everything except one thing — a trip to Helgi's childhood home.

Not one of Esther's relatives, Liisi or her three grown sons, her brother or his chaos of offspring, children and grandchildren, had wanted to drive Helgi and Esther to the place where Helgi had grown up. "There's nothing there," they had concluded, one after another. But there was more to it than that.

After the war, the Russians had lopped off all the land to the east of the Narva River. The place was officially in Russia now. No one, eager as they were to fulfill every whim of their Canadian guests, was willing to go. Esther hadn't pressed them.

Liisi's oldest son had found a friend who agreed to take them. Everything was possible for money, even though Helgi and Esther's visas did not include the restricted industrial areas of the north-east that they would have to travel through.

Esther assumed that the driver, whose shock of dark hair fell over his eyes, was older than her. His mouth seemed to rest in a grim twisted line, though when he smiled, which was rarely, the gloom lifted momentarily.

He was to do all the talking. Helgi and Esther had no quarrel with this. Helgi's Russian was rusty and Esther only knew a few words. Apparently his was perfect. They would pretend they were from Narva and just crossing the border to visit relatives. They would blend in with the busy traffic of others doing just the same.

Esther peered into the East, in the direction they were heading. Clouds were piling up, as if they too had to stop at the border and seek permission to cross. Esther ground her teeth and held back the sudden pulse of tears in her throat. She had felt like this since she and Helgi arrived ten days earlier: an inexplicable and burning rage, veined with such sorrow that often she had to look away from the people they were with. Estonians did not emote in public and Esther knew that a few tears would not be enough. There was no sense in starting. Especially not today.

Helgi's tension was palpable, a white-knuckled kind of anguish that seemed to bob in an even larger sea of something unnamable. Sadness? No, the word wasn't strong enough. A dismay? A kind of painful nostalgia?

Esther felt she was descending into the worst of all hells instead of going to her family's homestead. Even the sheltering sky turned dim and hazy, suddenly foreboding. No, she didn't want it to be this way. She couldn't allow it. Helgi needed her for once. Helgi needed her to keep the ship from sinking.

They drove into Narva and through it without a pause. The centre of town was old and lovely, like many of the other towns they had visited, but she didn't feel welcome. Her stomach was screaming, *turn back! turn back!* and all the horrific monsters of her refugee childhood seemed to throb in her skull at once. Were they crazy? What would happen if they were caught? Vague images of blowing snow and Siberian cold churned in her imagination as they approached the border.

The border post itself was just one small shack hunkered down at the side of the pitted road. There were a half dozen cars ahead of them, all dull and similar. Esther breathed deeply. Here, things were designed to be functional, first and foremost, even if they weren't and broke down often. Especially in Tallinn, where the massive rows of concrete apartments stood grey against the low sky, much of what was functional struck Esther as ugly. Was it her Western prejudice or just a stark contrast to her own image-obsessed culture? Esther worried the thought intentionally to keep her mind from the panic that was brewing in her stomach. It was important to appear calm. Nonchalant? No. Nobody here was nonchalant. A tense casualness would do fine.

Esther put her hand on Helgi's shoulder. Helgi squeezed it and let go. She sat back in her seat. The cars were passing through the post, one by slow one. Until it was their turn.

The driver spoke in rapid-fire Russian. The guard leaned forward, looked at Helgi and asked her a question.

Helgi nodded. He didn't bother with Esther. *Idite*, "Go!" he commanded. The driver pressed the gas pedal down as they exhaled. The world was different on this side, Esther noted. Different, yet the same. She could not put her finger on it.

It wasn't long before they turned off the main highway and headed north.

Almost fifty years had passed since Helgi, who was only in her early teens then, had left this place. Would she recognize the spot? Would there be a spot for her to recognize?

A village arrived quicker than Esther had expected it. She still wasn't used to the short distances of a small country. Helgi read out the sign in Russian for Esther as the driver slowed. The place was tiny, a nothing, just a few houses clustered at the side of the road and a ramshackle store of weathered wood that leaned to one side. Two old women, with their kerchiefs knotted at their throats, stood outside, gesturing broadly as they spoke, their hands pointing and dancing this way and that.

Helgi nodded for the driver to continue and then directed him right at the next cross-road. She asked him to slow down. He shifted down to first.

Fields. Everywhere, they were surrounded by fields of potatoes and yellowing rye. Helgi rolled her window down and hung her head out. Esther could see that Helgi was biting her lower lip and squinting to hold back tears. Was this it? But where was the house? The hedge of lilacs?

Helgi raised her hand, a gesture for the driver to stop. He skirted a muddy pothole and pulled over to the side of the narrow road. Helgi opened her door and stepped out. A breeze caught her hair and it fluttered in her face. She did not brush it away. For a long moment Esther watched her aunt while Helgi stood still, swallowing, swallowing. Again and again. Finally, she dropped her head and stepped away from the car.

The driver lit a cigarette. "I'll stay here," he said. Esther followed, wanting to come along but unsure if she was welcome. "Do you want me to come with you?" she asked.

"*Tule, tule.*" Helgi gestured without looking back. Esther took Helgi's hand and the two women walked in silence down the road. The wind whipped Esther's hair across her face, into her mouth and when she flicked her tongue to dislodge it, she tasted the salt in the air. The sea was close.

Beyond a line of trees, a faded house peered out at them. Was this it? As they neared, Esther saw that it was a Russian house, like her cousins had taught her, three blue-rimmed windows at one end. No, this wasn't it. When she and Helgi were only 100 metres from the house, Helgi pulled at Esther's hand. "Let's go over the fence here."

Esther used the fence post to steady her foothold on the wire. Helgi hiked up her skirt and took Esther's hand as she followed. The field was set out in neat rows of potatoes, ready to harvest. The leaves were spotted and yellow, drooping and dried around the edges. Helgi followed a furrow toward a copse of pines and poplars. Halfway there, she turned around, spread her arms out as if to show the ground around her.

"The house isn't here anymore. I'm sure this is the

spot. I recognize the trees," she said. Helgi looked like a forlorn scarecrow, battered thin by the wind. She stood unmoving, only her eyes alive, as if they were seeing what was no longer there: the mirror trimmed with oak leaves, the sideboard, the long cookstove that was built into one corner of the kitchen. Esther crouched to pick up a lump of soil. She crushed it between her fingers. Had the house simply fallen into disrepair, collapsed into the earth, or were there lumps of charcoal buried beneath the even surface of the field?

Helgi sighed deeply, wrapped her thin arms around herself and began to sway, softly, from side to side. Esther stepped closer, half expecting to see tears on Helgi's cheeks, but instead, there was a wistful smile, almost elfin in its sweetness.

"Come," Helgi said, surfacing from the realm of memory. "Let's go into the woods."

The wind calmed as they stepped into the shady grove. Helgi began walking around, scanning the ground, peering up into the branches of the trees, as if looking for some sign. She stopped at an enormous pine at the edge of the copse and circled it twice before she lay her hands on the coarse ridges of the bark. Esther turned away when Helgi laid her cheek against the trunk. She wandered into the copse.

Mushrooms were growing everywhere. It had obviously been wet. Esther didn't know anything about mushrooms except that Vanaema, Helgi and Sofi used to pick and can basketsful once upon a time.

This was the place. This was the place and there was no one to tell her about the mushrooms.

The thought caught in her throat with such clarity that Esther could not hold back her tears. Their years of exile were irreparable. The feeling had been growing every day and though Esther tried to push it away, it welled up in her as certain as thirst: Estonia wasn't Esther's home. And it would never be. Though her mother tongue filled some of the gaps, like a spring that finds crevices between rock, she did not belong to this place. Or not all of her, or even much. Not enough to erase the fifty years that her family had rooted in another place.

Esther unearthed a coppery yellow mushroom that was spongy underneath. Her fingerprints turned brown on its underside. When she broke it open, she found it was full of worms.

Helgi's voice rang out, calling her name and Esther turned to see Helgi, flushed and breathless, coming toward her.

"I found it. I found it. The tree's grown around it but if we can find an axe, I can get it out!" She pulled at Esther's hand without waiting for an answer.

"What did you find, Helgi?" Esther asked as she followed Helgi's long stride toward the neighbouring house.

"The ladle. The ladle I hid in the tree when Mamma and I buried all our pot and pans. It's still there. I want to take it to her."

The back door of the house opened before they

arrived and a plump, middle-aged woman wearing a flowered bib-apron stepped out to greet them. Helgi explained, half in Russian, half with gestures, that this was the place where she had grown up.

"*Moi dom, moi dom*," she said, holding her hand out as if to indicate a child, pointing to herself and then to the blank potato field. The woman nodded her head deeply and invited them in. The house was a jumble of plants and faded framed pictures. She gestured to a scarred wooden table and put a plate of deep fried doughy twists that had been sprinkled with icing sugar in front of them.

She pointed to Esther and Helgi and asked, "America?" They nodded and she smiled, broadly revealing many missing teeth. She poured them glasses of a deep red juice that was so sweet Esther could barely drink it.

Helgi gestured for a pencil and paper. On it she drew an axe and a ladle sticking out of a tree. The woman laughed and brought her a small axe from outside the back door, shaking her head, puzzled. She also laid a ladle on the table.

Helgi laughed, told her no, stood up, taking the axe and asked the woman to come with them. She followed them back to the copse. Helgi lead them to a birch that forked, about four feet off the ground, into three large branches. And there, in the cup of the tree, was a rusted ladle, embedded in the wood. Helgi let the woman look, then set to work, chopping away the edges of the wood around the ladle. Though

Esther offered, her aunt did not want help. She and the woman waited quietly until Helgi produced the ladle with its stem still ensconsed in a clump of wood.

"Mamma," she pointed to the ladle, "this was my mother's." Helgi's eyes sparkled and Esther could not tell if it was from joy or from tears that had yet to emerge.

They said goodbye to the woman, leaving their names and the words Winnipeg, Canada written on a piece of paper she extended to them. She wanted them to sit again, eat, drink some more, but they refused, pointing to their wrists, indicating they had to return to Tallinn. She gave them some of the twists, wrapped in newspaper, to take with them.

Esther took the ladle from Helgi, once they stepped back out on the gravel road. The tip of the handle, where once there had been a curve perhaps, or a hole by which to hang it, was rusted away. There was only one place, in the pit of the ladle bowl, where a few spots of enamel were left untouched by corrosion. Between the bowl and the end was the chunk of wood that Helgi had chopped away from the tree. It was still warm and a faint dampness emanated from the bare wood.

This was all that was left. The driver started the car as they approached. Esther gave Helgi the ladle and climbed in the back. The driver said nothing as he turned on the narrow road and roared back in the direction they had come.

Tomorrow, they would join the four million people

HELGI ◆ DECEMBER 1944

THUMPITY KLAK-KLAK, THUMPITY KLAK-KLAK, thumpity klak-klak.

I don't like this train. I don't like this train.

I don't want to go to Berlin. I don't want to go to Berlin.

I want to go home. I want to go home.

"Don't be stupid," Sofi says. "Can't you see there is a war? We left for a reason."

Sofi is so mean to me sometimes. Can't she see that I'm cold? My chest is seized so tight, it's as if my skin is too small for my body. My dress feels as though it'll burst if I breathe hard. I would like to see outside but the little windows along the top of the boxcar are too high, and Isa's not here to lift me, though he'd probably tell me that I'm too big anyway. I only hope that this warm wind doesn't melt all the snow and leave the ground bare and ugly while we're trapped in here.

I don't like this train. I don't like …

Mamma and I sit close together, on our suitcases, at one end of the dark boxcar. There are so many people that I can't see Sofi at the other end where she sits with the young mother she met in Danzig. We stayed the night there in an enormous and icy hangar filled with people, all of them running away, just like us. Everyone was restless to get a place on a train, but now that they're here, they're restless for the train to get somewhere, to be somewhere else. The wind makes it worse, I think. Who wants to be shut inside?

Two older men try to pry open the boxcar door. They push at it and pull until the heavy door finally gives. Its metal wheel screeches and resists as it moves along the rusty track. It leaves a sprinkling of red rust on the grey floor that shine when bits of sunlight fall there. Eventually, the wind sweeps the rust away.

A woman with a little girl comes to sit at our end to keep warm. Five or six people get up and stand in the doorway, all in a row as if they were going to jump. I get up and move too, closer to the door, to see outside.

"Helgi," Mamma takes my arm as I rise, "don't go near the door. If you fall out, the train won't stop to let you back on."

I step carefully between the people, finding spots among the baggage where the floor is not covered. If the train lurches, I don't want to fall into anyone's lap. There is a space against the wall opposite the open door, between a woman in a grey coat and checkered shawl and a bald old man. I squeeze into it.

There. Through the forest of legs in front of me, I can see snowy fields, a blur of white and grey, and sometimes a little green when we pass some woods.

At the station in Danzig, I told Mamma that I wanted to ride on top of the train but she wouldn't let me. "It's too cold there, besides, that's where the soldiers are." You can hear them — the men — moving, like angry bears on the roof, every time we slow down or stop. If it's this cold down here, they must be frozen up top. The wooden planks chill my backside. Emme's sweater only comes to my hips and then there's just my dress and stockings. I fold my knees up close to my body and pull the front of my sweater over my legs.

The wind is playing with the trees. Gusts catch their branches, and whistle through. I hear a loud crack — a branch has broken nearby. Did it hit the train? I'll never know.

Thumpity klak-klak, thumpity klak-klak, thumpity klak-klak, thumpity klak-klak.

The rhythm of the train makes me want to repeat my thoughts, to think in rhymes, to think aloud and louder still.

Where am I going? Where am I going?

I want to go home. I want to go home.

Can't go home. Can't go home

Emme, Emme, Emmemmemmemmemme …

I'm going to jump!

Thumpity klak-klak, thumpity klak-klak, thumpity klak-klak.

I want out. OUT. To pull my suitcase out from under Mamma and heave it out of the rolling train, then fly after it myself. It would be my raft, buoying me over the windy world below with only my legs dangling over its edge, the trees tickling the bottoms of my feet. My suitcase and I wouldn't thump into a ditch. No. We would soar to the undersides of the clouds, through them and to the top. I would step onto a cloud that looks like a bird, perhaps a goose, white wings spread wide to hold me and its neck reaching for tomorrow. I would stand on my cloud and shake my finger at all the stupid people who are part of this stupid, stupid war.

THUMPITY KLAK-KLAK! Thumpity klak-klak. Thumpity klak-klak.

The train can't leave me to my thoughts; it breaks in with a blare, as if it were going into a tunnel.

We're going to Berlin. We're going to Berlin. We're going to Berlin.

That's where Isa is! There was a letter from him in Leibau.

Thumpity klak — klak , thumpity klak — KLAK.

The train slows. Mamma says that there is never any good reason why or where this train stops; we go fast through towns and stop in the woods. Sometimes we stop to let another train by but sometimes, it just stops to rest. This time we stop in the forest.

Everybody moves at once. The woman beside me gets up and so do I. I don't need to pee but this is our only chance so I might as well go out. Mamma reminds me not to go far. You never know when the train will move again.

"Helgi!" Sofi calls to me loudly because all the people are moving and talking now and the soldiers are hammering at our ceiling with their bootheels. "Come help." She gestures for me.

Sofi has laid her coat down for the baby. It whimpers and starts to cry in hiccups as the girl undresses it. The child's face is tiny and shrivelled like a walnut. I see that the girl is crying too as she lays open the messy diaper. The baby has diarrhoea.

"Helgi will wash them," Sofi says to her but the girl doesn't look up.

Sofi turns to me. "Birute has no more clean diapers after this one. Can you go wash these?" she asks me. Still Birute doesn't look up. Sofi nods her head at me and frowns. She moves her lips without saying anything. What? She does it again. "Say yes," her lips are saying, "Say yes."

"*Jah* ... Where are they? Sofi, will you come with me?"

"In a minute," she answers. Birute looks up shyly and says, *dankeshern*. She gives me a newspaper package that is damp and smelly, and the diaper she just took off. The baby is screaming now, his face red and angry, and he struggles when she tries to wrap the clean diaper around him. I jump down from the car; the step is broken.

Mamma has already climbed down into the ditch that runs parallel to the tracks. Through a hole in the ice, she fills our water bottle. Beyond the ditch, soldiers are peeing in the woods, their backs turned to us while others call from the roof, bad words in German that I don't understand. I go up the track toward the engine so that I won't mess the water where Mamma is. The baby's cries fade.

There is no other hole for a while. Finally, I stop near the second engine and chip at the ice with my heel. It isn't very thick and breaks easily. The damp newspaper comes apart when I try to open it so I drop the bundle of diapers in the water whole. With the toe of my shoe I push at them until the water turns a sluggish yellowy-brown.

Does Kadri have a baby too? They took her to the hospital in Danzig straight from the boat because her pains had started. Mamma and Sofi went to see her but they didn't tell me anything. Sometimes they treat me like a child.

I reach into the water to fish the diapers out. It is so, so cold. My whole body seizes the chill and my chest throbs one sharp stroke. For a minute, my breath escapes me. When I find it, my eyes water. I won't cry. I won't cry.

One by one, I scrub the diapers and rinse them out as best I can until my fingers are so red and cold that I can barely feel them. Sofi comes to me.

"Thank you," she says. "Birute is too ashamed to

ask for help but the baby is sick. He's so young."

I nod. Sofi goes a bit further and makes her own hole in the ice. She takes a newspaper package out of her pocket and opens it up. I finish the diapers. As I am squeezing them out, I walk toward Sofi to see what she's washing. She doesn't look up. The water is red. The water is red. It's blood.

I back away, then run. As I pass my hole, I grab the diapers and run away. Back to our boxcar, I run, avoiding all the people. The soldiers are standing beside the train now, smoking and ignoring me. I have to go down into the ditch to get by them. Blood? Does Sofi have tuberculosis too? I climb into the car.

I thrust the diapers at Birute and go to Mamma. "What is wrong with Sofi," I ask. "Is she sick?" Mamma frowns and her forehead is suddenly full of deep lines running this way and that.

"Blood, Mamma. Sofi was washing blood from some rags." The lines in Mamma's face soften. She looks from side to side, as if to see if anyone is listening. What are they hiding from me? More people climb in the car, talking, waiting for the train to leave again.

"Don't worry," Mamma whispers. "It's just Sofi's time. I will tell you about it soon. Not here." She pats my cheek like I'm a child. They never tell me anything. I'm thirteen already, I want to shout. She pulls me down to sit on the suitcase next to her and puts her arm around me. The train lurches suddenly. Voices shout from the roof and more people jump in. A man helps Sofi onto the train when it is already moving. I

FALL 1989 ◆

THE FIRST GREY DAY IN WEEKS. COOL TOO. ESTHER was relieved. It was hard to justify her desire to hide away in her room when the golden leaves of fall glinted in the Indian summer sun. Brenda had lured her out for a few walks along the river since Esther's return from Estonia, but as soon as Esther was home again she closed back in on herself, like a screen door with a spring, snapping shut.

Eighteen months: this was the longest Esther had lived in any one place since she left her parents' house. And what did it add up to? A foam mattress on the floor, boards and bricks for shelves, a stack of milk crates for her clothes. Only her desk qualified as real furniture. And the furniture only reflected another, deeper impermanence. The trip to Estonia hadn't solved any of the problems that Esther hoped it would. Rather than filling in the blanks that had always existed, the trip had posed more questions. More questions that she couldn't answer.

Esther poured the last of the mountain ash liqueur she had brought with her from Estonia — a farewell gift from a cousin — into the flowered teacup on her desk. The liqueur was the only thing she had unpacked. Her suitcases lay in the corner of her room, exactly where she had dropped them two weeks earlier. They were bulging with presents for the rest of the family; picture books, knitted mitts and scarves, two strings of amber and a stiff pile of flowered linen tablecloths. The whole family had been so pre-occupied with Kadri's crisis that Esther had managed to avoid the inevitable task of distributing the loot.

The sweet, thick liquid slid down her gullet. It was sugary, almost unbearably so, but Esther had grown to appreciate it. What she liked most was the liqueur's fragrance, a mossy, woody smell that caused her nostrils to flare, and drew tears into her eyes. It was as if the liquid in the brown bottle with the faded label was a distillation of her trip — familiar and yet foreign. Esther licked the brim of the teacup.

What would she do now that the bottle was empty? Who would she be if she wasn't Estonian? Esther's sister Kadri didn't seem to have that problem; no, but she had others.

While Esther and Helgi had been away, Kadri's life

had erupted. Kadri had moved into Helgi's house to take care of Vanaema and Bob had been left in charge of the boys. He had grown frustrated with their demands and antics after two days and insisted that Kadri return home from Vanaema's to "her job". Something in Kadri must have snapped because, for once, she had refused. She had swooped down on the marital home, took the boys by the hand and ushered them over to Sofi and Elmar's.

Over the three weeks of Esther and Helgi's absence, Sofi had grown progressively more anxious as she realized that Kadri and Bob were not talking, not kissing and making up as husband and wife were supposed to. She had even pleaded with Esther, on the way home from the airport, to talk to her sister.

"And what am I supposed to tell her?" Esther had asked.

"That families are meant to be together. She needs to apologize to Bob. Tell her, Esther. Tell her," Sofi begged.

"Why?" Esther had been intransigent.

"Because something bad will happen if they don't. Please."

"Just what would happen?" Esther asked.

Sofi eyed her younger daughter with panic. "Children need their fathers. You don't know anything about these things. Wait till you have kids of your own."

But Esther hadn't talked to Kadri. Helgi had taken on the role of Kadri's confidant. Kadri was still at Helgi and Vanaema's and the boys were still with their grandparents.

It was time to get going. Vanaema was expecting her for dinner. She downed the last of the syrupy liqueur. The flavour always lingered for a long time afterwards, coating her tongue, disguising the sourness underneath.

The three women — Kadri, Aunt Helgi and Vanaema — were gathered around the kitchen table when Esther arrived. The small room was imbued with a sense of heaviness that not even the odour of baking cabbage rolls could disguise. Esther sat in the remaining chair and took Vanaema's hand in hers. Vanaema smiled absently and squeezed Esther's hand.

Helgi broke the silence. "Sofi's coming over." There was no need to say more. The pot was brewing. They didn't have to wait long, but they each waited with all their attention, listening for the car to turn into the driveway.

When they heard Sofi arrive, Kadri, Helgi and Esther stood up, went to the living room, and Vanaema pulled the oven door open to check on her creation. Esther stood against the wall, as far from Kadri as she could get.

Sofi's row of curls was twisted and wiry about her face. Her cheeks blazed and her small eyes zeroed in on her eldest daughter, Kadri. She crossed her arms over her ample bosom and began.

"This can't go on, Kadri. You must make up with Bob. The boys have been with me for almost six weeks now. It's not that I mind them, no, I enjoy them, they're good boys, but I've raised my children. Elmar's too old for this. They tire him out. We're supposed to be retired. And you? What are you doing to fix things with Bob? Nothing. Nothing!"

Kadri, who was usually demure and compliant, at least outwardly, in the face of Sofi's tirades, looked around her as if hunting for an escape route. Finding none, she faced Sofi squarely. "I'll come get the boys right away," she said, clenching her hands.

"And take them where?"

"That's my business, isn't it?" Kadri's voice was rising, ever so slightly, with a new edge to it. She looked to Esther as if to ask for backup but Esther only shrugged. She had hoped they would leave her out of it. Esther's battling days with Sofi were done. And had Kadri ever backed Esther when she was the one on the hot seat? Sofi's voice rose a half octave.

"Your business? Your business?! You've left the twins with me for over a month and suddenly they're only your business? Have you lost your head, girl? They're my grandsons too and you're my daughter. I want you to phone Bob right now." She marched past Esther, who pulled herself flat against the wall, and took the phone from the receiver in the kitchen. She extended it to Kadri.

"No."

"Sofi …" Helgi interjected, standing up from her chair, uncertain but determined.

"Sofi what? You haven't helped any by letting Kadri

stay here at your house. Let me deal with this. You don't know anything about marriage."

Helgi sat back down, stung by Sofi's attack. Esther wanted to rush to her aunt but knew that she would be stepping into the line of fire herself. And, pressed against the wall, she wished she could be absorbed into the paint, to avoid the oncoming storm. Esther realized too, that there was a part of her that hadn't grown up and left home at all. She'd just run away.

"Phone." Sofi's command drew Esther back into the fray. Sofi stabbed the humming receiver at Kadri.

"No." Kadri's voice had a tone of defiance that Esther hadn't heard before. "Maybe I don't want to go back to Bob. Maybe I want to take my sons and go out on my own. Did you ever think of that?"

Sofi obviously hadn't. Kadri's words stunned Sofi into momentary silence. She had lived with Elmar for thirty-five years in spite of their differences. Though he wasn't perfect, wasn't the person who she had imagined she would marry, at least he was stable. He'd never hit her. He always brought his paycheque home. What more could you ask for? Esther knew that Sofi put a lot of stock in just having someone, as if she was terrified of being alone. Was it the war that made her like that? Or her generation? Maybe both.

"Families are meant to be together," Sofi began more quietly and then, building steam again, added, "you have children. What stupidity are you talking? Huh? How will the boys live without their father? And how will you support them?"

"This isn't a Communist country you know," Kadri was pushing her advantage. "Didn't you come here so you could do what you wanted with your lives? Have some choice? Not be told what to think, what to feel, where to live?" Kadri stood up to her full height, her chin in the air. "Or doesn't freedom apply to me?"

Sofi was dumbfounded, clearly thrown off balance by Kadri's line of argument. No, Esther and Kadri weren't supposed to use their parents' anti-communist rant against them. Sofi's arm dropped to her side. Esther took the receiver from her hand, where it had started buzzing with rhythmic squawks. When Esther turned the corner into the kitchen to hang the phone up, Vanaema was standing in the middle of the floor, her eyes glazed, lost.

A lull in the storm drew Esther back into the living room. Kadri was gathering up her purse, her keys and her jacket, her jaw set and fierce. Sofi's eyes were wild.

"NO!" Sofi shouted. "You can't. You can't!" she repeated as she rushed toward Kadri, grabbing the strap of the purse. The two women, mother and daughter, locked eyes and looked as though they would stay that way, frozen and unreliquishing, if Vanaema hadn't intervened.

She came from the kitchen brandishing the rusted ladle with the chunk of wood around its centre, shouting in her small voice louder than Esther had ever heard her shout before. "Leave her be! Juhan says to leave her be!"

And Sofi let go, sunk back into the couch, her head

in her hands as the front door slammed shut. As Kadri's car started up, Sofi began to sob and nobody knew what to do. Helgi sat next to Sofi, patting her back distractedly. Esther lead Vanaema back into the kitchen, guiding her to sit down. Who was Juhan? It was no time to ask. Esther sat down herself and let her head fall into her shaking hands.

SOFI ◆ DECEMBER 1944

HOW LONG ARE WE TO SIT IN THIS TRAIN STATION?

"Until there is a train," Mamma answers though I don't think I even asked my question aloud.

If only I had something to do. Everyone is nodding quietly, Mamma holding her cheek and Helgi with her gaze stuck on some distant planet that only she visits. I pat my pocket to make sure Isa's letter is still there and get up from my chair. The high ceiling echoes back the sound of its metal legs scraping the marble floor. The people at the other tables, all waiting, like us, open their eyes to see if anything has changed.

It's just me. It's just me, go back to sleep you sorry people. Women with children, babushkas and moustached old men slouch over tables, with their backsides stuck to the green metal chairs. Hungry children are whining but I can't do anything for them.

We've been in this drafty cavern of a Berlin train station for twenty-four hours already. And Mamma has turned crabby from her toothache. There is no one to help her here and nowhere else to go. The tracks toward Bavaria have been cut by bombing and until they're fixed, we can't go south or anywhere else. In Bavaria there is an army hospital where we might be able to get work enough to put a roof over our heads and food in our stomachs.

Birute's milk will dry up if she doesn't get something to eat soon and then the baby's screaming will never stop.

I pick through the sad cardboard suitcases and faded rucksacks made from sugar sacks and pillowcases. A low iron fence separates the restaurant from the main station, and somehow, it makes us invisible to the morning passersby. My legs are stiff from all this sitting. I stretch them, one and then the other, as I walk toward the wickets at the far end.

Berlin. I've dreamt about this city before. But not like this. What would it be like to be going to work, putting on a clean dress and taking the train to an office? A steady stream of smart businessmen and women in ironed clothing come from the street, cross the cavernous room, and clatter down the wide stairs. Where are all these people going?

I lean over the railing of the stairwell and see a

woman coming up, slowly, as though she has a headache she doesn't want to disturb. She's wearing a bright green dress with padded shoulders almost as wide as a doorway. Her turban matches the dress and her cream-coloured clutch-purse matches her shoes. At the top of the stairs she pauses and looks toward the restaurant beyond me. She's beautiful, but I can tell that even she has troubles. There are mauve bags under her eyes. Sleepless nights, perhaps, worrying about the war that they are losing? As she walks away, I see that the dress has a small slit in the back and that just above her dress line, near the stocking seam, is a hole that's been darned.

I watch her walk away and then lean over the railing again. The waiter told me the stairs go down to the underground railway.

But where does the underground railway go? I finger Isa's letter in my pocket.

There is an older man to my left. I'll ask him. "Excuse me," I smile at him and practice the German phrase in my head, "where does the underground railway go?"

"Everywhere," he snaps and turns away. But where is everywhere? In Isa's letter he said the camp where he was being sent was near Berlin. Nobody seems to want to tell me. If only Kadri were here.

Kadri's laugh makes people do what she asks. It got us onto the ship in Latvia, out of the seige in Leibau, and, in between her pains, it got her to the hospital in Danzig.

Of course, it couldn't save the baby. Last time we saw Kadri, she had no smiles left. She was so pale and still that she reminded me of her carpet roll under her hospital bed.

"Take it with you," she had said, nodding toward the carpet. "No Kadri, you keep it. You'll be needing it." I couldn't take it. What did she think was going to happen to her? I just couldn't.

I didn't want to leave her but Mamma said we had to go on. Kadri said so too. I don't think my smile will ever be as pretty as hers. Nobody smiles as wonderfully as she does, not even Zara Leander, and she's in the movies.

Now, that's something I would like: to be in the movies. I can act. I'd be good.

A tall man in a grey suit with pant legs so wide that you can barely see his shoes comes to lean against the brass railing next to me. He unfolds his newspaper and starts to read. He looks nice enough. Maybe he'll talk to me.

Bitte, "Please sir, do you know where this place is?" I smile and pull Isa's address out of my pocket. He's older, in his thirties, but quite handsome with a nice straight nose and lovely eyebrows. I would like a baby with eyebrows like those.

"This is at the edge of the city," he says, after a second, without looking at me.

"Would you be so kind as to tell me how do I get there?" I ask, just for something to say, and try to catch his eye.

He gives me directions but barely glances in my direction. "Is it far?" I try coax him into conversation, "I'm new in Berlin."

"Two trains," he repeats flatly, "and you change at _____ ."

"*Danke*," I say a little too loud. He looks back down at his paper, dismisses me like a schoolgirl. Everyone is so rude these days.

I wander toward the stairwell so that he thinks I'm really going. But what if I really did go find Isa? I step down the first step. The marble stairway is wide enough for ten people across. I run my hand along the well polished brass railing. Imagine, here I am in Berlin — Berlin!

I walk down the stairs slowly, like they do in the movies, one foot at a time and never looking down. I wonder if they ever trip? I wonder what an underground train looks like? Mamma won't let me go anywhere. It's not fair that there's nothing to do but go back and forth between the restaurant and the information wickets. Besides, if I go see Isa, they'll be so glad that I've got news of him.

And I'll be back before they notice I've been gone. Besides, the trains aren't going anywhere. They won't even miss me. I look back up the yellowed marble stairs and wonder about Mamma and Birute. Mamma will just tell me I can't go.

I won't be gone long. At the bottom of the stairs there's a wide platform down the middle, like a regular station, except the ceiling is lower and the air smells of mildew. I sneeze very loudly and people turn to stare. I step close to the edge and look down the track. Nothing coming. Which direction am I going?

There is a young woman, maybe twenty, a bit older than me anyway, who is standing quietly nearby. She is wearing a brown coat and shined brown shoes with heels. Mine are so scuffed — it's been so long since they've seen shoe polish.

"Please, miss. I'm going to the ———— station. Which way is that?" She puts her index finger to her lips to think and looks up. Her eyes are very big and brown, like her coat, shiny, like her shoes.

"I'm not sure now, but I think it's the same way I'm going. This side. If you don't mind me asking, where are you going?"

"To see my father. He's at this address." I fish for the paper in my pocket and show her.

"That's this way. Yes. I'm sure it is. If you don't mind me asking, where are you from?"

"No, it's okay," I say. Happy day, someone to talk to. "I'm from Estland, Estonia. And you?"

"I'm just from here, I mean Berlin," she smiles. "But that's not very interesting."

"Oh no, yes it is," I assure her. "Do you live by yourself or with your husband?"

"Oh no," she blushes. "I live at home. With my mother and my grandparents. Do you have a husband? Or are you alone?

I laugh. "A husband! Where would I find a husband now? I'm only 18, you know." I lie a little so she won't think I'm just a baby. "All the boys my age are fighting. I had a soldier friend in Estonia but I don't know where he's gone. I'm here with my mother, my sister and a friend. Do you have a sweetheart?"

"No. I don't either." She bites her bare lip and looks at her shiny shoes. I wonder if she can see her reflection in them?

"My friend is married though," I say and the girl looks up again. "She's Lithuanian and has a baby — but she doesn't know where her husband is either. Maybe in Germany. Birute and I met in Danzig." My stomach twists a little.

"Where are you going then?" the girl asks.

"We're trying to go to Bavaria but the line is broken."

"Oh, I see, but ..." the girl starts to ask me something else but her voice is drowned out by the bellow of the long train as it bursts into the station.

"This one is ours!" she shouts over the squeal of the brakes. We step in and find a seat. The train is nearly empty. At our end, there is only a woman wearing a heavy fur stole who has tried to bury her wrinkles in too much makeup. I nudge my friend and point.

"It's fox," she whispers with admiration. The train roars through station after station. After a while, my friend leans over again, "Your German is good, you know. Did you learn it in school?"

"Yes, I did and from the soldiers in the hospital where I worked. The wounded, you know. I helped the nurses. I'm going to work in a hospital in Bavaria too. I want to be a nurse."

My friend gets up suddenly as the subway pulls into the station. And then she's gone.

I get up and walk the length of the car, past the made-up lady and down to the far end where an older woman and two spotless children sit. My stomach growls and the woman stares at me. I look back at her and she turns away. I should've smiled. Maybe she would have given me something to eat.

My station comes up. I get off and clamber up the cement stairs. The air chills as I approach ground level and I pull my coat shut. It's too tight. So is my brassiere.

Fresh cool air fills my lungs when I step out into the light. I breathe in deeply. The outdoor platform is raised above the street and there are houses on both sides, white, stucco houses with red tile roofs, and a bakery on the corner. Everything looks so crisp in the winter air. I haven't been outside since the last time the train stopped on the way to Berlin from the transit camp and I had to wash my rags in the ditch.

Nobody's looking. I open my coat and lift up my arm to smell myself. I stink. And I can still smell that awful stuff they made us shower in when we got to Danzig. De-loused, indeed! We don't have lice. Then they didn't even leave the water on long enough to wash. What I would have given to wash properly, with soap, and have a fresh dress to put on.

I wait twenty minutes for the train. Mamma must be worried. I should've said something, but it's too late now.

I ride three long stops before I get off. The houses are sparse here and somehow shorter and stouter than the ones in town. Empty lots, filled with clumps of big trees, span the spaces in between. There's no one on the platform to ask where to go. At the ticket wicket I show the woman behind the cage my slip of paper. She talks slowly and curves her words strangely, but at least she doesn't tell me not to bother her. She must get lonely working out here.

I head down the wide road that she pointed out. It feels good to be away from the crowds and to be moving. I take long strides and stretch my stiff muscles; the cold air feels alive inside of me. Only the sun is missing.

I hum to myself as I walk. What are the words to that song the soldiers always sang, especially after Kadri came to see them?

Vor der Kaserne, vor dem grossen Tor steht eine Laterne und steht sie noch davor ...

It was about a woman named Lili Marleen. Sofi Leppik doesn't quite have the same ring. I'll have to marry someone with a wonderful name, like the movie star Willy Fritsch, or Hans Albers. Sofi Fritsch ... ? Sofi Albers — oh, I like that, but you can hardly pick a man just because of his name. He has to be good looking too. And tall, at least as tall as Isa.

Isa, Isa, Isa: where is this camp?

Vor der Kaserne, vor dem grossen Tor ...

I almost walk past the gate of the camp, it looks so much like the other buildings around it, only that there is a small sign. The gates stand wide open and there is no guard so I walk in and across the courtyard to the biggest building. There, the sign *Büro* hangs on the double wooden doors. I gather my courage and step into the dim hallway. There is an open doorway on my right and the clatter of a typewriter.

"*Bitte*, I'm looking for my father," I say to the woman there. "His name is Juhan Leppik."

"A second please," says the young woman at the typewriter without looking up. She's wearing a brown suit and while I wait, I look for badges to see if it's some kind of uniform.

"What is his name?"

"Leppik, Juhan. He wrote to us in Leibau to say that he was being sent here. That was four weeks ago but he was only in Danzig then … "

She rifles through the papers in a filing drawer. "*Nein*, he's not here," she says and slams the drawer shut.

"Then where is he?" I ask. "How will we find him if he's not here?" The woman looks annoyed. I smile at her but it doesn't come out right because suddenly, I want to shout at her. "Doesn't it say where he is? Was he here and then was sent away?" She stamps back to the files irately and pulls one out.

"I don't know. Go talk to Sgt. Kuntz." She doesn't tell me more than I ask. Where do I find this man?

"Please," I begin and she turns to me with her lip curled. "Where is this Sgt. Kuntz?"

"Do you think we don't have anything better to do

that keep track of a bunch of *auslanders* who don't have the sense to stay home?!" Her face is pink with rage and I back out the door, back out into the open air. I turn to run.

How will Isa find us? I take a step down and my ankle turns on the front stairs.

I fall forward, scraping my knee. I hit my elbow, scrape the palms of my hands on cement. Ow. Right away it stings.

Kurat! "Damn!"

When I look up from my bloody knee, a man in a fine wool suit is standing over me.

"Fraulein," he says curling his lip but offering me his hand, "you must be more careful."

"And you!" I start in Estonian without thinking, "What about you bloody, goddamn Germans. You've lost my father. You've lost my father. I hate your stupid war." I hear myself shouting but can't stop. "I hate all of you … "

Two men in uniform rush out, talking urgently and break my tirade. I get up without his hand, smooth my skirt and turn my back on the man. He says nothing. They never have anything useful to say. Never. Nothing.

Idiots. Idiots, idiots, idiots, I say to myself all the way back to the station.

Where is Isa? Idiots. Isa will find us. Idiots. My knee smarts. The underground takes me back to the station, back to Birute, the baby, Helgi and an angry, black-eyed Mamma.

◆ WINTER 1990

ESTHER TUCKED THE NEWSPAPER UNDER HER ARM as she climbed the smooth, wide stairs to the hospital. She pushed open the heavy glass doors and made her way across the lobby to the elevators. She and the Ukrainian receptionist exchanged nods — no, Esther wouldn't stop and gab today. There had been nothing about Estonia in the papers for such a long time that even all the other Eastern Europeans at work had stopped asking her what was new. It was as though, with the introduction of the plan for entrepreneurial independence — the IME — in the new year, Esther's tiny Baltic country had ceased to exist. The small link she had forged with her trip, severed. What was new these days was The Wall and The Wall. The newspapers were thick with it, chunks of grimy mortar even appearing at London auctions.

Esther found Vanaema near the nurse's station, sitting quietly with her hands in her lap, watching the passers-by. Her head bobbed and, in her hands, she cradled her dentures like a baby bird that had fallen from a tree. No, Vanaema had no idea what was happening in her old world. She didn't even recognize her family some days. She had slipped so far into a world of her own over the winter that Helgi was the only one who could consistently unlock the door and help her back out.

Vanaema had slipped on the wet kitchen floor and broken her hip on a glum November day when Helgi hadn't come home until late. Her accident had lodged the door to her world in its frame and left Esther's grandmother barricaded inside.

Esther swallowed at the lump in her throat and kissed Vanaema's soft, wrinkled cheek. The old woman's lips turned up in a secretive smile as she murmured something beneath her breath. Esther leaned closer, turned her ear to Vanaema's mouth. Words, yes, but their rhythm was somehow not familiar. She listened for a while, Vanaema's butterfly breath on Esther's cheek, before it struck her: Vanaema was speaking in Russian.

A knot clenched in Esther's throat again. Would Vanaema recognize her today?

She took her grandmother's hand and patted it, calling, "Vanaema, Vanaema," hoping that the

Estonian would remind her who Esther was. It was the only language they shared. Her grandmother looked up.

"*Sofi tütar*," her grandmother stated.

"Yes," Esther answered, relieved. Sofi's daughter.

"I named her after my eldest sister," Vanaema continued in Estonian, as if she had been thinking these very thoughts when Esther interrupted her, "but little Sofi was never as level headed. My oldest sister," she said, sitting taller in the straight-backed vinyl chair, "was beautiful, wise and strong. She had a long dark braid that hung down her back like a rope. Sometimes, when Leoni went to play with the neighbourhood boys instead of me, she'd undo it and let me brush it. Oh, it was even softer than the cat."

Vanaema patted her lap, as if to remember a long ago cat who had sat there. Her hip was on the mend but she wasn't strong enough to go home yet. Esther came to see her every week, at least once. More than anything else, it was Vanaema who kept Esther from quitting her job and leaving Winnipeg, like she had been thinking of doing. Everytime Esther came to the hospital, Vanaema would have some new story about another relative, long-lost for sure, but part of her history nevertheless.

So Sofi, Esther's mother, was named after Vanaema's sister? Did Sofi know that? Esther turned back to Vanaema, who after a pause, continued her story. "I named my baby after my sister Sofi because she was the strongest. I wanted for my girl to be strong too.

My sister Sofi used to bring big trays filled with soup bowls to the table for our visitors. The Baron and his men. They came with their howling dogs to go hunting on the grounds my father kept for them."

Vanaema paused and slowly lifted her frail arms up above her head, as though they were rising on their own accord. "He was a big man. Very big and wide."

She paused again, as if to recall the Baron, and her eyes glazed over. Every week there was a surprise. Esther had no idea that her family had dealings with the Russian aristocracy. Not that it mattered, now, beyond curiosity. Esther had always maintained, in the face of Sofi and Elmar's Estonian fanaticism, that what mattered was the present. And in the present, Esther was not happy with her job or her life. The trip to Estonia had crystalized a feeling, the feeling of wanting to be closer to the soil.

Vanaema stirred. She put her teeth in. "It was the Baron who was so big. But he was kind too. Leoni was a little afraid of him but I wasn't."

"Sofi used to put me up onto the long wooden table after the meal was over. The men would balance on their stools, sipping something warm and full of smells while they puffed their cigars and pipes. Oh, our kitchen would fill with their smoke and it would linger in the house for weeks after they were gone. I liked it even though my mother used to complain."

Vanaema halted midstream. Her face fell in on a deep frown. Was she thinking of the soldiers who came and got Leoni? Esther nudged Vanaema gently, to urge her on. She wanted to hear it all. While there was still time.

Regret stabbed at Esther's chest. If she left now, she'd miss the rest of the stories. There was so much to catch up on. How long could she wait? There would always be something else to keep her from going. Brenda was right. She needed to take charge of her life. Just go. Get in her car and drive West. Find that woman who had talked about perma-culture. Find the place where she fit, if such a place existed.

Esther wanted to tell Vanaema that she was going and that she wouldn't see Esther for a while. Would it be as hard for Vanaema as it was for her? Helgi knew already. And though she didn't say so, Esther knew that her aunt would be sad to see her go.

Kadri, on the other hand, still elated over her new found freedom, had urged her younger sister on. "Do it. You won't regret it. It felt so good to finally stand up to Sofi," she had said. But Esther had been standing up to Sofi for years, hadn't she? The more Esther looked at her life, the more she saw that there needed to be more than just resistance. She needed to take hold of her life and actually become who she wanted to be.

Now all she needed was the courage to let go of Vanaema, the courage to deal with Sofi and Elmar. Sofi would blow up for sure. Ever since Kadri left Bob, Sofi had folded in on herself and there was a desperation in her attempts to bring the family together, though nothing had really changed. Sunday night was still Sunday night. Now that Bob was gone and the old country was newer in their lives, they had reverted to speaking in Estonian. Even the boys had picked up a few words.

Esther patted Vanaema's pliant hand again. "Why did your sister put you up on the table?" she asked.

"I was the entertainment, you see." The old woman giggled and spread her hands, as if balancing herself at some height above the ground, as if, at this very instant, she was entertaining the Baron and his men.

"What did you do, Vanaema?"

Vanaema continued, with glee in her voice. "One time the Baron laid a golden ruble on the table. Usually it was only a few kopeks but this time it was a big, glowing coin. I couldn't take my eyes off it. Even Leoni, who usually hid under the table while this was going on, came up to see it. I remember how he put his chin on the wood and couldn't move his eyes away."

Vanaema's eyes sparkled and she rubbed her hands together. She herself seemed to glow in the bland fluorescent lighting of the hospital.

"This, he said to me, will be yours if you can button up your coat. He had seen my sisters buttoning my coat every time I wanted to play outside. Earlier that day he had said, "aren't you big enough to button your own coat? I was four but with so many sisters, Leoni and I were pampered. We were their little dolls."

"My fingers were so short and fat and I remember how smooth those buttons were. They slipped between my fingers but I pushed and pushed and worried them through the slits in my coat, one by one. The men talked and laughed, drinking out of the bottles they kept in their jackets, and clapped every time I got one button in. My mother, Sofi and all my other sisters looked on from the edges of the room. And, do you know, the ruble gleamed like a cat's eye in the dark. I wanted it so badly."

Her grandmother stopped, suddenly lucid, and looked up at Esther. "I buttoned my coat and I won the ruble but I didn't see it again until the night my father took me to Estonia in the rowboat. I hid it in my shoe. Only when I was older did I find out that that one coin was equal to what the hunters paid my father for many months of work." Vanaema sighed.

Esther took her grandmother's hands in hers and squeezed them gently. Vanaema looked at her again.

"The Barons were so much richer than we were. We had enough, but many of our neighbours didn't. All they wanted was enough land to feed their families."

Enough land. Something so basic, so simple. Simple, and still, this is what Esther wanted too. Only now, it was there for the buying. Anyone could have land in Canada, couldn't they? The era of Barons and Tsars was over. All farmers had to contend with now was the bank.

And then, Vanaema said something that Esther would think back on for years to come. How did she know? "And you, Sofi's daughter, you are going away too. The ruble kept me safe through all the years, the war, the trip to Canada on the ship. I don't need it anymore. You take it."

Vanaema leaned over slowly and pulled off her shoe. She picked it up and sat up straight. She pulled the insole loose and tipped the tiny, worn loafer heel down. A fat coin slid into her hand. Vanaema's hand closed over it before Esther caught more than a glint of the gleaming metal. Why did Vanaema want to give it to her?

Esther began to protest, not knowing why. The coin seemed like an enormous gift and burden all at once. If Vanaema gave it to her, she would have no more excuses, no more reason to evade her future. Would she be able to create a new life for herself, as Vanaema had done, over and over again?

Vanaema reached her fist out over Esther's lap. Her small hand held the treasure tightly, like the roots of a tree around a rock. What did Vanaema expect her to do? Esther looked over and saw that her grandmother's eyes were screwed shut as fiercely as her fist.

No. No, she couldn't take it. What if she failed? What if she didn't find anything out West. What if she reached the farm whose address was now inked in her blank book among her cross-sections and floor plans, stayed for a few days and then could think of nowhere else to go, nothing else to do? What then?

Suddenly, the hand over Esther's lap burst open and there on the map of Vanaema's palm, the ruble beamed, like an eye.

MARIA ◆ MARCH 1945

"FRAU LEPPIK!" THE VOICE OF THE BIG WOMAN
whose long smelly hair spills out of her armpits cracks
the air. She lives three bunks down from Sofi, Helgi
and me at the Ingolstadt hospital.

"Frau Leppik!" she hammers. "Your Sofi has been
in the toilet for over five minutes now." She speaks to
me in a broken German that rattles. She knows about
as much of their harsh language as I do. We've all had
to learn a little, enough to get by. Enough to buy our
scraps from the local shops. And enough to make sense
to each other.

The big woman stands in the gap between the bunks
like a false tooth and blocks out the light. We
abandoned the window side of the room for the back

wall. The windows have no curtains and, in the winter, there were terrible drafts. The new workers always get the window side, but at five months we are among the old timers.

"Frau Leppik!" she insists. When I stand up, the top of my head comes only to her chin. I must be the smallest woman here. For once, to be small is a good thing. Less food needed. More of my portion for Helgi.

"Jah, jah," I tell the woman and push her aside and go see what Sofi is up to. Sofi, Sofi, Sofi. What has she bartered for lipstick this time? Whose stupid idea was it to put the mirror in the toilet?

There's so little space. Everyone is always pushing, looking for more room, more privacy. A bit of clean. What people live like this? Auslanders: foreigners. People without homes, is what we are. Twenty of us in one room smaller than a stable. Twenty to share one bathroom. How does a person belong to herself in a place like this?

I don't even have my own name anymore. We dropped the "a" from Maria when we bought my Estonian papers, so now I am Mari, an Estonian woman. In every way. It's better like this. The stories we've heard from the Russian camps are enough to make "a"s fall out of the sky. The Russians are not allowed work, like we do, in hospitals. And their camps are said to be places much worse than this. Hard to imagine.

Our space, not home, is two bunks wide with forty

centimetres of floor between, crammed beneath the sloping eaves. Who lives like this for two years? Who?

"It used to be a school," Frau Galunas told me, "a primary school. One of the soldiers said so." Frau Galunas' bunk is next to mine. On the bottom. She's Lithuanian and a few years older than me. A Latvian girl who is Sofi's age, eighteen, sleeps up top. Sometimes she and Sofi chatter into the night. We have to tell them to be quiet again and again.

Frau Galunas and I talk too, but softly. She is alone here. Her sons are with their father in another town where they all got work together. There he can keep watch over them. There is no work for boys at the hospital and no place for them to stay.

"If only Janis was a few years younger," she told me one night, "then he could be with me. You are lucky to have daughters."

"Jah," I whisper back in the darkness, "but what of the soldiers? So many bad things have happened to our girls here."

And my Sofi, already a young woman, wanting boyfriends, swirling her skirt in front of the sentries. Oh, she does not want to listen to me or anyone.

I am not halfway to the toilet to get Sofi when the air raid sirens screech.

UUUUUUuuuuuuUUUUUUuuuuuuUUUUUUuuuuuu
UUUUUUuuuuuuUUUUUUuuuuuuUUUUUUuuuuuu

Sofi bursts out of the toilet, upper lip red, the other bare just as the big voice pounds down.

Achtung! Achtung! he screams.

Achtung of course, stupid man. After more than four years of this we know already. The aisle fills up, people pressing toward the door.

UUUUUUuuuuuuUUUUUUuuuuuu

"Achtung! Achtung!" The smell chokes me. It's a slaughterhouse smell, like when we butchered pigs. The siren sounds like a pig too. High and torn, like a baby in pain. Haven't had even a finger of pork for months now. From the hospital kitchen we get nothing but thin soup and coarse bread. What does that cook do with our rations? I shouldn't be so hard, I guess, because even the stores in town have no meat. Not even pork ears, tails or feet. A meat ration card is as good as the Deutschmark. Coloured paper. Even cigarettes won't buy anything anymore.

Everyone pushes toward the basement. I don't need to walk. They carry me between their thin bodies, my nose stuck among armpits and chests. I can't breathe. It's always like this. Down the stairs. Three flights. From the stairwell we hear the planes coming and we hurry down. It's dim here and full of hot breath, reeking with the rancid smell of empty stomachs. Sofi with the Latvian girl from the next bunk. But where is Helgi?

Sofi, kus on Helgi? I ask her. *Ei tea.* "I don't know," she shrugs. The corners of the shelter are dim. Helgi is so thin and quiet these days, even more than usual, that it's easy to miss her. The soup is making us all sick. All three of us vomited two nights ago. There was no bucket for the bedside. One after another we had to run down the dark aisle, ducking clotheslines. We string them up inside at night. Too many things have been stolen from outside. Frau Galunas lost her only dress. She saw the woman come and take it but there were soldiers outside and she couldn't run after the thief in only her underpants and brassiere. She pounded on the window and screamed but no one could understand what she was saying until it was too late.

When she calmed down she was able to explain. In German. I sent Sofi to look for the woman but she was long gone.

"Helgi ... " She is in a corner, quiet. "Where have you been?" I scold, my fear draining into relief. The worry never seems to stop. And Juhan: fifteen kilometres away from us, in the train yard. At least he won't be sent to the front. We made his papers too old for that and nobody has questioned him. The past few years have left their lines on his forehead, like notches on a stick. When was it that we were young?

Juhan doesn't get any days off. If we want to see him, we need one whole day to walk there, visit, and walk back. Today was the day. Sunday. Planes on Sunday. War doesn't even pause for God. Certainly not for families to visit. I move closer to Helgi as more bodies squeeze into the shelter.

The whiz of the bombs barely carries to here. Good. They are far. Maybe more being dropped on the factories in Juhan's town, though for what reason, I can't imagine. Everything is flattened there already he says. His workplace was bombed last week. Flattened one whole wing of the train hangars. Fifty workers killed. He was throwing out some garbage and hid in the garbage ditch. Went back to his barracks when it was all over.

"Mari." Frau Galunas is beside me. She has never called me by my Christian name before. She is shaking, arms flapping, head bouncing.

"Eva?" I think that this is her name. I beckon her closer and take her under my other arm as she squats down to be with Helgi and me.

"Eva, be calm. Nothing is wrong. The planes are going away. It'll be alright." But they don't. I can hear another wave of them coming, of bombs whizzing. Eva's skin is cold and slippery. I can feel bones everywhere. She is wearing the dress that Sofi and I made for her. We tore her pillowcase for the top and made the skirt out of the lining of her coat.

Eva is shaking like a boxcar, almost rattling. I sing to her softly.

"Eva, Eva," I begin and stop. It's the Russian lullabye that my mother used to sing to me that comes into my mouth. Eva is too upset to notice. I begin again, making up Estonian words for the tune as I go.

Eva, Eva,
kallis, kallis
päike loojab nüüd,
Eva, Eva,
helde, helde
maga unede käes.

It doesn't even rhyme. Oh well. Eva's shaking calms eventually. We stay in the shelter for an hour and a half. Helgi, Eva and I hum to ourselves, huddle, wait for the safe sound while Sofi paces like a bear in a cage.

When it finally comes, UU UU UU UU UU UU UU, short and flat and rhythmical, we all go back up above the earth, slowly, slowly. Out in the daylight again, people talk almost as if nothing has happened.

More of the same. Always more of the same. And now, there's no time left to go see Juhan, to find out if he is still alive. Another week to wait. This waiting is so familiar too. For years, I waited to hear from my family, from that house on the other side of the border where Leoni and I had grown up in the shelter of our sisters. But nothing. Ever. Not even to this day.

It is dark already. The days cannot grow longer or warmer fast enough. This winter has been the hardest yet. Less food, less clothing, less patience. Less will.

◆ ◆ ◆

Monday morning I am awake before sunrise. Like every morning since they pulled my tooth, I tongue the gap between my molars. Now I have two spaces, both on one side where air can chew air. One of the doctors put my pain to an end with his pliers.

I sit up and see that everyone else is still sleeping. We all sleep like squirrels in hibernation after a raid day even though only our beating hearts have been busy the day before. The cement floor is cold through my shoes, even though I have kept them warm under my blankets. Though I haven't looked, I can feel how the ruble has sunk into the heel. Where will I keep my coin when the shoes are gone?

I can see my breath. The bathroom is free for once. Not having to wait is a small, but sweet, blessing in this life. Imagine — this is what luxury has become. Being able to use this dirty hole with no one behind the door to pound my waters out. Although we wash it twice a day, throwing water on the walls and floor, I don't trust it. There is no soap. The toilet seat is long gone. I squat on the rim of the bowl and pee. The other comes out in a thin pea-soupy stream. The usual now.

I walk back through the tangle of clotheslines to our bunks and reach up to smooth my hair. My hair, my hair — all the wave and shine has gone from it. It thins weekly. Juhan, from his height, notices it.

Mari, su juuksed. "Your hair. I can see your scalp in places." He caressed my head, my cheek. The girls looked away. They are not used to seeing us touch.

Juhan: now another week to wait before we see him. At least he was healthy last week. Frau Galunas' — no — Eva's youngest had an earache when she last saw him. They don't send for the women unless someone is nearly dead and sometimes not even then.

Not even then.

Monday mornings are my time to go into Ingolstadt to look in the stores. It is almost six. If I leave here now then I can be back to the hospital by 8 a.m. I take my string bag from under my mattress and feel for the two packages of cigarettes in my pillow. Good. I put them in the bottom of my string bag. I touch my chest. Yes, the gold chain with my wedding ring is there too. Juhan would not let me barter it away, but, but if there was something good, I would trade it. I would. If there was something good. God would understand.

I take my panties from the line next to our bunks. As long as it is warm enough, I sleep naked to save them and wash them out each night. They are almost more hole than cloth but they dry out quicker now. I put them on, drawing my skinny legs up through the two biggest holes.

Sofi is still asleep, but Helgi's eyes are open, big and underlined with a purple as dark as plums. Her stomach will not hold the food, especially not the soup. It's nothing more than potato skins, rancid butter and beet tops, it's so thin. I give her half my bread. It runs through too.

"Helgi," I touch her forehead. She is warm, almost feverish, every morning now but what can I do? "I'm going to see if there is any food." No one stirs at the sound of my voice. Helgi nods. To overhear each other would be as disgraceful as putting your ear to the wall. It is harder to keep your eyes to yourselves but we pretend not to see. Not to hear. Or feel.

"You stay inside. Away from the soldiers." I whisper in her ear.

The soldiers are getting meaner every day. They are losing the war. They don't tell us this but we can feel it. We don't know who is coming. The English and the French? Americans? Someone said that some of the Americans are black like tar. I don't care who comes. Only that this war be over. Unless it's the Soviets. Only that I don't fall into their hands ...

"We will go back to Lithuania, when the war is over." Eva told me late one night, her voice full of tears.

And us? What will there be left of our home? I stroke Helgi's head and go.

Down the echoing stairs, out the double front doors, I close them behind me. Down the front steps of the two-storey red brick schoolhouse, across the yard to the gate where the sentry sits. He doesn't look at me as I pass out onto the road. The Germans like big, chesty women. I worry for Sofi who wants a husband but the soldiers barely look at Helgi or me, unless we are in the way. Sometimes, I am pushed out of lines or spat at, "Auslander!" There is not enough food to go around.

The street is grey. The morning is grey and barely lit. I walk quicker than these short legs should carry me and play with the new gap between my teeth. My legs are used to keeping up with Juhan's long stride. The stores usually open at seven, sometimes earlier, but there is nothing in them. Why do I go? Like a sheep. We must go. What else is there? Sometimes Eva comes too. This morning I let her sleep. She looked sunken and dead in her bed.

It's four kilometres to the centre of Ingolstadt. There are some farms along the way and they all have big dogs — shepherds — to keep us away from their empty fields. What do those dogs eat? I walk in the middle of the road and the dogs stay quiet.

Closer to town, I feel other movements around me, but I don't see anyone until I am at the butcher's. My first stop. The fat German woman who works there uncovers the windows. A blob of white paint covers a yellow star of David. The Jews were gone before we arrived. The woman uncovers the glass cases inside too. I think of how it must have been before, laden with kosher meats, chicken, gefilte fish. No pork; they don't like pork the way we do. I can see from outside that there is nothing today, as usual. I turn to go but the woman opens the door.

"*Guten Morgen,*" she says. I nod. She is the same woman who is here every week, her cheeks so pink they hurt to look at. She's wearing a different dress than last week but this one is old and fading. Maybe even a bit loose? She gestures for me to come inside. Is there something that I didn't see?

She slides open the glass case and takes out some green sausage. It will make us sick again. I shake my head and turn to leave.

Warum? "Why?" she asks, an urgency in her voice. I see that she looks over her shoulder into the back room and then at me again. I hold my belly and pantomime throwing up. I don't know why I do this. We have never spoken to each other before.

"Kommen," she whispers, beckoning me closer to the counter. And again, *"kommen!"* I go. She looks around and disappears into the back room. The store is so big with me in it alone. I look out towards the street. Should I run? What does she want with me? I hear a cooler door open and close. Then footsteps. I wait.

She comes carrying a piece of sausage. Beautiful. As thick as my wrist and pink like her cheeks. It is about twenty centimetres long with big, white chunks of fat in it. I swallow. I don't move. I don't understand. I show her my bare palms. I forget my cigarettes, my ring on the chain and the coin in my shoe.

"Nein, nein," she reaches for newspaper and wraps it. I don't understand. Still. What does she want of me? The rustling of the newspaper crackles in the stillness. I can smell the sausage. There is someone on the street. Is Helgi coughing? What does she want? My heart pounds like bombs dropping on my chest. My knees feel watery. Suddenly, I feel hunger like I have not felt it for months, maybe years.

She leans across the counter and reaches the package toward me. I step back, dizzy. Her voice is as loud as God's.

"Take it. Take it quickly before anyone comes. Take it!"

Still I hesitate, *"Warum?"* Nothing is for nothing. I

have nothing.

"My sons …" She bites her lower lip and tries again, "All this killing …" She lifts the package.

I step toward her as she thrusts the package into my hands. Nothing has ever felt as heavy. As she turns away from me, she mutters, "We are both mothers." I hear her run into the back room, her slippers clicking on the tile floor. The store echoes. Suddenly, I remember my ruble. It is still there. I put the sausage in my string bag. I leave.

I walk. I do not go to any more stores. I do not look at anyone. There are more people in the streets now. I want badly to clutch my bag against my chest, but I don't. They must not see. They must not know. I walk back to the hospital quickly.

I can think of only one thing: there is meat for Helgi. There is meat for Helgi, Sofi and me. There is meat for Helgi, Sofi and me. And Eva. Yes.

LATE SPRING 1990 ◆

KADRI AND THE BOYS HAD LEFT AFTER DESSERT. HELGI slipped away to help Vanaema wash and get into bed. Both of them were staying over at Sofi and Elmar's so that they could see Esther off in the morning. When Elmar disappeared to tinker with some last minute repair on her truck, Sofi cleared her throat. Esther and Sofi sat, alone, in the living room.

"I'll do the dessert dishes," Esther offered, standing up.

Sofi was quick to her feet. "No, no, there's not enough. I'll do them in the morning."

Esther sunk back into the armchair. What did Sofi want of her? She had barely spoken to her daughter since Esther had announced in a quavering voice that she was quitting her job and going to British Columbia in the spring. The blowout Esther expected had not materialized. If anything, Sofi had descended further into the gloom that had plagued her ever since Kadri left Bob, and Sunday dinners had become increasingly tense and silent. No, now that Kadri had defected, Esther was not going to step into the good girl's shoes, even if there was room for her there, for once. It was too late.

Sofi broke the silence. "I understand ..." she began, her voice trailing off. "When I was young, I wanted to have my own life too, I didn't think of my family."

"I do so think of my family," Esther countered.

"What I mean is ..." Sofi stumbled uncharacteristically, "... is that doing what you want isn't everything."

"Are you trying to guilt me about leaving?" Esther stood up. "I can't believe it. Give it a rest, mother."

"Why is it that I'm always the bad mother in your eyes? Why can't you listen to me for once. I tried so hard," she stifled a sniff.

"Who said you're a bad mother?" This was leading nowhere constructive that Esther could see.

"You and Kadri always go to Helgi. She didn't sit up with you all night when you were feverish babies, or sew your clothes for you, or take you to lessons. She always had the easy part. Bringing you toys. It's not fair."

"You're not a bad mother, Mamma." Esther said it firmly, in hope that Sofi would not challenge her. "Is this what you want to talk about the night before I go? Really?"

"You're going because of me, aren't you?"

"No." What else was there to say to this? Esther rubbed her temples. She had hoped that they could spare themselves the old sparring, the jostling for power. "I'm going because of me." It seemed so cliché, but it was true. Would Sofi allow herself to see that?

"You can't trust anybody except your family." Another volley. This one didn't come as a question.

"And?" Esther took the bait.

"People will hurt you. They'll take advantage of you. You won't find what you're looking for."

With this, Esther lost her level-headedness. What did Sofi know about what Esther wanted? "Why?" she pleaded, leaning toward Sofi with her jaw set, "Why can't you encourage me just for once? You've always told me I can't, I shouldn't, that it won't work out, that the boogey monsters will get me. Why, just for once, can't you see that this is hard for me and that I need your encouragement, not your constant criticism. And don't tell me that Estonians don't praise; I am so sick of hearing that." With this, Esther could no longer hold back her tears. She fled to her old room and as she turned to thwack the door shut behind her, she heard Sofi sob.

A few minutes later, Sofi was at her door. Esther said nothing to her red-eyed mother as she stood in the doorway. "People die when you go away, you know. We might not be here when you come back,"

Sofi said, stepping back to pull the door shut before Esther could ask what she meant.

In the morning, Helgi and Elmar helped Esther pack the last of her gear into the truck. Sofi emerged from the house only at the last minute, when Esther was already behind the wheel, her hand on the gearshift, the motor humming. She came to the window, leaned in to kiss Esther's cheek, whispered, "Good luck. I love you." and pressed a rigid plastic card into her hand. Esther placed it on the dash without looking at it and mumbled "thanks," putting the truck in reverse.

Only later, when Manitoba and half of Saskatchewan had flown off the rims of her wheels, did she see what Sofi had given her as a parting present: a phone card with Sofi and Elmar's number raised above its surface. The widening distance between Esther and Winnipeg — or perhaps it was the stream of sappy country tunes that inhabited all the channels of the radio — had opened a gap in Esther's armour. Suddenly, she regretted that she hadn't told Sofi that she loved her too.

She clicked the radio off, popped open the lid of the cooler on the seat beside her and fished in the densely packed coolness for another bag of carrot and celery sticks. This was the only food Esther had packed for the journey herself. Helgi had done the rest, with suggestions from Vanaema, when she surfaced from her reverie: a jar of homemade dill pickles, the last bag of Vanaema's pirukad from Helgi's freezer, a lump of Gouda, a fat finger of sausage, two Polish weiners to boil for dinner over her propane campstove, mustard, two conspicuously white hot dog buns, a half dozen boiled eggs, a package of cold cut sandwiches — probably mortadella and peppercorn salami — on seedy, dark rye. In a string bag behind the seat were three apples, three pears, and a dozen plums. Everything in multiples of three to correspond to Esther's planned three days on the road. Behind the seat were three cans each of peas, sauerkraut and beets, salt and pepper shakers and a large box of Shreddies. She'd only have to buy milk along the way.

Esther pushed the lid shut and pulled down the visor. It was getting unbearably hot and now that the sun was leaning into the West, her eyes began to ache. She hadn't slept much the night before. Between her own anxieties and the lingering effect of Sofi's words, she had flipped like a pancake all night until she was rubbery with sleeplessness.

Esther's eyelids tugged downward. Perhaps she should pull over, take a nap in the shade. But where was there shade? The prairie spread out around her, its undulation unbroken by any tall growth. There were no houses close to the road and the only sign of life had been the occasional farm dog, sniffing out the perimeter of its territory. There was certainly no place to cozy in and sleep. It would have to wait.

A few kilometres later the road dipped suddenly without warning into a deep coulee and, in its pit, a small creek snaked black through a twisted strand of trees. Esther pulled over.

She retrieved her sleeping mat and straw hat from behind the seat and spread the mat out on the dry earth. She wriggled until her hips fit into a comfortable groove and then adjusted her hat to keep the contingent of descending flies off her face.

Between the broad sweeps of transport trucks and cars on the highway, the air fell silently around her. When she closed her eyes, her body felt as though it were still in motion, rolling forward over the beckoning landscape, into slumber, forward, forward.

And then the truck is behind her, parked in the darkness. In front of her a house.

Light
Esther, go
Tock, tock, tock
Wooden stairs beneath her feet
The door opens
A kitchen, familiar chairs, cupboards
But it is bare
A shadow falls
A blanket of heaviness
She turns to run
Away
Flings the door open and he is there
A man, his mustache heavy, his eyes yellow
He reaches for her
NO!
His mouth gapes
He reaches again
Yells "One family, one uniform!"

NO!

Esther sat up and put her hands across her pounding chest. And breathed deeply until the panic subsided.

The shade had moved and left her lying in a pool of her own sweat, hot. Two noisy ravens circled above, wondering perhaps whether Esther would be dinner. She got up slowly, wiping at the curls that had stuck to the nape of her neck. She rolled up her mat and shook her head to clear it.

The man in her dream. His voice was still with her. One family, one uniform, he had screamed. Esther shook herself again, as if to cast off the voice and the memory of his gaping mouth and his terrible eyes. One uniform: what did he mean? Which uniform did they wear? Which destiny? The bare house? The man in pursuit?

Esther climbed in her truck. The circling ravens flapped away disappointed as she turned the engine over.

SOFI ◆ MAY 1945

ROUND AND ROUND. I WILL DANCE FOREVER. THE war is over. Is over, over.

The Russians are in Berlin, in Estonia, but I'm here in Bavaria, with the Americans.

The Americans, the Americans, they all look so well fed and washed. And tall. I want an American to marry. And we'll have three beautiful children who will do exactly what I tell them to.

Round and round, I'm not going to find one at a Polish dance. No, not here, we're the lost ones, the shabby ones who haven't got a home to go to. An American wouldn't want a girl who eats potato peels out of the garbage. But I won't tell them that. Do they need to know?

I can dance and sing. I used to know how to cook good things, holoptchi, cottage cheese cakes, and hot Nothings, twists of crispy fried dough with powdered sugar sprinkled all over, all over the dough, the kitchen, and the front of your dress.

Maybe there'll be some more food now. It's been potato peels for too long.

Round and round, I'm getting dizzy with nothing in my belly. "Wait," I say to my partner, whose name I don't even know, "my head is spinning. Let's sit down."

He takes me by the elbow, firmly but gently and leads me to a chair at the edge of the hall, making me pause when we nearly collide with other dancers and then propelling me forward again when the way is clear.

"*Danke,*" I say to him in German. I don't speak Polish. He sits down beside me. He gives me his hand to shake. Oh, a gentleman.

"Peter." He offers his name like it were a roast goose on a silver platter.

"Sofi," I answer back as politely, sitting up a little straighter. "I'm from the hospital. I work there as a nurse. That's what I'm going to do now that the war is over. Be a nurse. I'm from Estonia. Are you Polish, Peter?"

He laughs gently, though at what I don't know. "Yes, I'm from Poland. Aren't you tired of sick and wounded bodies yet?"

"But the war is over. It will be different now. I want

to work in the maternity ward, helping babies to be born. Do you like babies?"

He laughs again.

"What is so funny?" Is he laughing at me?

"I thought you were feeling sick?"

"Yes ... ?"

"It's just that you seem to have recovered quickly."

"Yes ... ?"

"Never mind," he says, patting my knee in a very brotherly way, "tell me about the kind of hospital you want to work in."

"It would need to be very big, many many storeys high and modern. Like they have in America, you know ..."

We talk for I don't know how long, him — Peter — asking me questions and me talking. He barely tells me anything about himself and when I ask why he laughs and asks me to come dance with him again. He is at least twenty centimetres taller than me. At least.

Another man, moustached and drunk, tries to cut in, to steal me for a dance. Peter steps aside to face him, holds onto my elbow and asks me if I'd like to change partners. The other man pushes closer, grabs my other hand, but his eyes are on my breasts. I pull my hand back suddenly.

"No. I'm dancing with this gentleman this evening," I say and take hold of Peter's shoulder again.

It is far too late when I remember that the Americans have made a curfew of 9 p.m. It is then that I notice that all the girls from the hospital and everyone from the hospital where Mamma works now have gone. I stop spinning.

I stop in the middle of the dance floor. The band keeps playing, the trombone sliding lower and lower, and the accordian sounding suddenly too happy.

"I've missed the curfew," I say out loud. "I've missed it. How am I going to get home? Oh no. Peter." I turn to him. "How am I going to get back to the hospital? It's on the other side of town. The military police will catch me. They put you in a cell for the night. With rats. And prostitutes." I turn away from him without waiting for an answer.

Where is my coat? Where did I leave that stupid purse of mine that doesn't have anything in it anyway?

There. Good. Maybe if I go right away, I'll miss the patrols. Yes. That's it. And I can tell them I was visiting my dying mother if they bother me. But what's the English word for dying?

Oh, I can't go. Prostitutes. Probably bugs in those cells too. What if they take me there? Mamma will have my head. I didn't tell her I was coming to the dance. She never wants me to go anywhere interesting. Take care of Helgi! Take care of Helgi! She's big enough to take care of herself for one evening.

I spin to see Peter right behind me. "I'm going now. Hold your thumbs that the military police don't catch me."

"I'll come with you," he says.

"No. It'll be worse for you. They might even shoot

if they see a man. With me, they'll only, they'll …" I can't say what they'll do to me. He'll think I'm cheap.

"But it's my fault too. I kept you here too long. I want to help you get home, Sofi."

"No. It'll be worse for me if they catch us together. Spies. Sabotage. You know. They don't ask many questions these days." It's only been three weeks since the armistice. They say that there are still Nazis who haven't surrendered their arms. "No. Absolutely no. But thank you for offering." He's too good to be true.

He walks me to the door, out across the wide yard in front of the hall. Only a week ago this was a POW camp. There's still barbed wire curled across the top of the fence but the gate is open and it's only a thin, sleepy Pole who guards it. Peter walks me to the fence and then a few steps down the road.

"You have to go back now," I order him.

"*Jah*. It was good to meet you Sofi. Will you come to dance again?"

I nod my head and turn away. At least twenty centimetres and even if he is Polish, he's quite nice looking. A nice man.

I hurry along with my head down. Sometimes, if you don't look at someone, they won't see you either. If I go a slightly longer way, around the centre of town, maybe they won't catch me. Good plan, Sofi, good plan.

I pull my coat closed. The nights are still cool though the days are getting hot under our tight roof in the attic. We need to get out of there. They've lost now.

We don't need to work for the Germans for nothing anymore. The Americans are in charge now.

A car? I jump into a dark doorway. The car doesn't turn down my street. I don't see who it was. My heart is pounding. I need to eat more if I'm going to dance so much. My knees feel watery. I cross my arms across my chest to keep my breasts from bouncing. They're sore. Will I get my period back now? Where will I find rags? I would rather it waited some more.

Stomach. I pat it as I hurry down the road. Don't bleed yet. It isn't time.

I turn the corner. Suddenly, I am caught in lights. No. No. It's too late to turn around. Why didn't I hear them? One shouts from the window. He tells me to come, in English. I walk slowly toward the jeep, its big white letters — MP — glaring. Oh, Sofi, Sofi, Sofi, what kind of trouble have you got yourself into this time? Military police trouble. Just smile nicely, girl. Just smile nicely.

"Girl," the driver says in English, hanging his arm out the open window. There too, the white letters blaze from the black armband. The other MP beside him ducks lower to see my face. "Girl, don't you know it's after curfew?"

I only understand girl and curfew but the rest doesn't matter.

I muster up what little English I have. I smile at them. "I sorry. Mmmmm. Mamma. Sick."

"Likely story. Get in the back." He points behind him to the back seat.

"No. Please, no." I pull back but the driver jumps out and opens the door for me. He points for me to get in. What can I do? I climb in and pull my skirts out of the way of the door.

"German?" he asks me once he gets back in.

"No. Estlander." The passenger soldier perks up, says something to his friend. I hear the word "young." They argue a little, not like fighting but trying to agree.

The passenger one, a blond with a small flipped nose, starts talking to me. At first I don't understand. I think he's speaking American though it sounds different. Then he points to himself.

"*Suomalaine.*"

"You're Finnish?" I ask back in Estonian. Suddenly my heart feels lighter. I breath deeper and lean forward. A Finnish boy won't put me in a prostitute's jail.

"You know it's after curfew," he says to me. I haven't heard anyone speak Finnish since we left home, but I still understand. Everything.

"Yes, I know," I answer back, talking half in his language, half in Estonian, "but my mother is very sick and I lost track of the time. I'm very sorry. I just want to go home. I live at the hospital over by the Danube. You gentlemen must understand," I add quietly, as if to take him into my confidence.

He smiles, touches the tip of his nose with his finger and gestures at the other man. I don't know what this means, but I wait. They talk for another few minutes before he turns back to me and says, "we'll drive you there. You'll be caught again if we put you out to walk and the next patrol won't have a Finn in it." He smiles a beautiful row of straight, white teeth.

They take me directly home. Just before I get out, I ask him, "How come you're Finnish and an Ami too?"

"America is a land of immigrants," he says, "and both my parents were born in Finland. I'm from Wyoming."

I get out and close the door behind me. Halfway to the gate, I look over my shoulder and wave to them. The driver scowls but the Finn waves back. Where is Wyoming? At the gate, the guard's mouth hangs open in astonishment and then he gets an ugly gleam in his eye as if he understands something that isn't there to understand.

"They caught me and gave me a ride home," I say to him and sweep past. I don't care what he thinks anyway.

I creep into the attic quietly. Only Helgi is still awake, like usual. I touch her head, it's hot. She gestures for me to come close.

"Mamma came. She brought a letter from Isa. It's under your pillow. I told her you went to visit a friend. I'm glad you're home safe."

I grope for the letter and climb into bed. I can't wait til morning to read it. I light the kerosene lamp and turn it low.

Kallis Mari, Sofi and Helgi,
I am in Munich. I am out of uniform. An old man

like me can blend in with the crowds and not draw any suspicion. The streets are badly broken and many buildings are only rubble but spring is flowering anyway. In the gardens where I sleep, there is a lilac bush and its fragrance makes me dream of our old garden.

Be careful.

Pay attention to the curfews Sofi. We have survived the war. Now we have only to survive the peace, he writes, as if he's been here watching me.

Helgi rolls over up top. She peers over the edge of the top bunk.

"Isa found us."

I smile up at her. "Sleep for once, will you?" She nods and sighs, disappears back to her bunk, the entire frame of the bed creaking as she moves.

I have met some people from home who have talked to the Refugee people already. They want to set up an Estonian camp — a house close to the train station — where they will live until there is somewhere else to go. I will try to get us a space there too. Everybody's looking to find a place to live.

Sofi, listen to Mamma and take care of Helgi. You are my girls and all we have left is each other. There will be time later for your adventures. I send you all much love. I wish I were there with you. In time, in time.

— Isa

I clutch the letter in my fist as sleep pulls at my eyelids. We're going to be with Isa again. Soon.

WINTER 1991 ◆

ESTHER CAUGHT HER STRIDE AS SHE ROUNDED THE stand of young firs where the path turned up toward the creek. Her skis made a zipping sound as they slid across the dry glittering snow. And lungfuls of chill morning air tingled in her chest. This was the way to begin a day. Winter birds squabbled among their snow-laden branches and the occasional coyote skulked at the edges of the woods. Thank goodness the bears were sleeping. And Justin too.

Esther made a point of getting up before Justin and often left him with his long arms flung across the empty bed as if she might still be somewhere there, between their lovers' sheets. It was important to greet the day on her own, to meet it as she was, her mind empty of radio chatter and her own swirling thoughts. This was the time of day when Esther had the world to herself. Of the five land members, only Louise rose as early as Esther did. But she had gone to Brazil for the winter. Esther missed her.

Of all the people at Seven Sisters, it was Louise who had known how to welcome Esther; in the moments when Esther felt like the stranger that she was, Louise had drawn her back in. It was Louise too who had shown her the clump of seven enormous birches that grew as one family, their roots intertwined, near the front gate. These were the trees that lent their cooperative land its name. In human terms, the Seven Sisters were actually three sisters and two brothers, none related in a biological sense. It didn't seem to matter that they weren't real family, Esther often thought, or maybe it even made life easier. She wasn't sure.

Often, when Esther passed near the gate where the white-barked giants grew, she would climb into the cup between their heavy trunks and recline, the dried leaves crackling beneath her. Their unrelenting permanence awed her. And yet, when their leaves turned brilliant yellow against the blue autumn sky and began to shed, Esther could sense the magnificence of their change too.

The leaves were long buried in the snow, the Sisters' dark arms bare against the wild sky, the cradle of their boles filled with snow. Winter was less bitter in the mountains than it had been in Winnipeg. Esther was still surprised by the stillness, the absence of the searing wind. Winter had a different flavour here; the darkness and snowed-in mountain roads inspired people to hibernate and burrow deep into their houses.

Houses: the word didn't quite fit the funky cabins that Martin and Honour had built back on the back forty. Louise and Gerta's place, which perched on the precipice of the creek gully, was small but solid. And Justin's place ... Well, it was a house. He had designed the two-storeyed, many-winged, wooden building with a huge passive solar sun porch on the south side and had built it himself. He liked space, or perhaps it was that he liked to fill up space. Justin did that well; every nook, alcove and room of the house had his imprint, the extra long bathtub to accomodate his height, the high kitchen counters and the stereo system that was wired into each room. The baskets, one at the foot of his bed, the other in the living room, for Roger, his scruffy, flop-eared spaniel.

Esther hadn't consciously chosen to move in with him. It just happened. Somehow. He had courted Esther through the summer, cooking dinner for her, inviting her along when he and Roger clambered up into the mountains above the land. Not that Esther had noticed his intentions. It wasn't until he demanded a kiss from her, barring her way across the huge fallen cedar that spanned a creek, that his intentions became clear. Justin? Attracted to her? He was so sure of himself, knew so much, could do anything. And Esther? It didn't bear examination.

Even as the thought clanged into obstacles in her brain, she let go and followed him.

They had become lovers in September and, as the weather cooled, he had enticed her in, bit by bit, starting with her books.

"Your pages will curl up if you leave them in your tent. Trust me. I know these things. It's getting damp." He cleared a space among his wall of tomes on Doing It Yourself, solar construction, alternative energy, green politics, Tom Robbins and Kurt Vonnegut Jr. novels. Esther's own tiny collection filled but a half shelf with a row of fat plant identification manuals and her growing collection of blank books for writing and drawing.

It wasn't long after that bears descended onto the land for their annual fattening on fruit. Neither the abandoned old trees nor the carefully pruned plum and apple trees where tin pie plates were hung to ward off the beasts, had been spared. Esther had heeded Justin's suggestion and brought in her cooler and box of dry goods. Next, she moved her clothes in and, finally, after she had slept in Justin's bed ten nights in a row, she packed up her tent and moved in completely.

Esther slowed her pace. The trail climbed here, just steep enough to warrant a sideways ascent. Some mornings she flew up the incline, her wooden skis clacking against each other as she scurried up, the squirrels scolding her fiercely as she went. Other mornings, like this one, she placed one ski next to the other purposefully. Esther felt weighted and her breasts were tender; PMS no doubt.

It would be just for the winter, Esther had told herself when she moved in. Just for the winter. If she stayed, if they wanted her to join Seven Sisters, she'd build herself a cabin, maybe up here. There were some nice rocky spots above the gully close enough to where the valley opened out to get good sun. She'd have to ski in and out in the winter but that didn't bother her. She liked the idea of being tucked out of sight, slightly inaccessible to those who didn't know where to look. Unseen.

Esther reached the top, puffing, her white breath hanging suspended in the still, sharp air. From here you could see the main valley and the place where the creek that crossed Seven Sisters joined the river. A thin slip of vapour hung over the aquamarine curves of the river as if it too intended to flow out to the Pacific. The valley often seemed like a place before time, or outside of it, as if the demons of the world had not discovered the beings that dwelt there. Winnipeg was far away and the homeland farther still. At the land, people's attention had been focussed on the situation at Oka and Esther realized, for the first time, that she too was living on occupied land. But what to do? She didn't belong anywhere else either. Did the Russians who lived in the Baltics feel the same way? Was there a way both they and she could live on another people's land respectfully?

Estonians wanted — no, expected — Russians living

in Estonia to learn Estonian. What could she, Esther, learn in North America, a continent of thousands of indigenous languages? She didn't even know what Sinixt, the language of the people who had inhabited this area, sounded like. Many had died of smallpox, deliberately infected by blankets. The miners, loggers and settlers had chased the rest away, south of the border, and the government had declared them extinct. Assimilate or die. That's what the Soviets wanted Estonians to do too. But would they succeed?

A possible war was brewing in the Middle East and the political situation in Lithuania was precarious but the radio muttered nothing about Estonia. It was easy to forget, for days on end, that Estonia even existed. But no, eventually something, a sound or smell or even a dream, would remind her of her roots.

Her dreams had been surprisingly clear of her usual demons. Would they eventually catch up? Not if she was careful, not if she hoarded her happiness close to her chest, let nobody know that she was contented. And when a distant voice tried to insist that surely Esther had no right to belong, she would tell it to shut up.

"Shut up!" Esther shouted, exhilarated. "Shutup shutupshutup!" The winter sun blazed on her nose. How good to be alive.

Freckle time. Especially after a few weeks inside, trapped by blizzards, her pale skin would spot, even in the weak mid-winter sunshine. Esther remembered how Elmar had called them sun-kisses when she had come home crying after the neighbourhood kids had teased her about her freckles. "It means the sun loves you," he had said and she had stored the explanation away as armour against the further, inevitable teasing.

Love. Odd. Had Elmar actually used the word love? It was hard to believe. She had so few childhood memories of him. It wasn't that he wasn't there. No. He was just quiet. Nothing like Justin.

Esther pulled off her Estonian mitts, one of the pairs that her Estonian cousins had knit, and rooted in her pocket for some dried apples. The leathery strips of fruit fought back when you chewed them. Esther liked that. She had become a vegetarian at Seven Sisters and what she missed most was the texture of meat, its resistance between her teeth, the way her jaw muscles had to work.

It was almost seven months since Esther had seen her family though she called every Sunday night, after dinner, when those who wanted to talk to her would come to the phone one by one. Sofi wanted to get an extension so that both she and Elmar could talk to her at once. Esther wasn't sure this was a good idea but she held her tongue. Sofi was far enough away; she wouldn't be able to interfere. Besides, Esther kept the important details of her life to herself. She didn't even tell Helgi that she was living with Justin, though she had wanted to. It was just that they'd see more in it than Esther intended.

What would they think of Justin? He was a prairie boy with family roots deep in the CCF. In Sofi and

Elmar's eyes, the NDP were as dangerous as Communists if they weren't actually Communists. He was eight years older than her. His brown kinky hair was long enough to tie into a small ponytail. At least he was tall. How had Sofi, with her obsession with height, ever managed to marry Elmar? Esther had frequently wondered what had drawn her parents to one another. Did they love each other? Esther wasn't sure. She picked a piece of apple out from between her teeth and pushed off.

Did she love Justin? Or was she in love with him, or something like that? Esther didn't know. She definitely admired him. Justin was a generalist. Capable. He took up space and never questioned his right to it. He talked a lot, but unlike Sofi who wanted to plot and plan the lives around her, Justin talked about the world, pulling apart what he read or heard on the radio and then reassembled the information in a way that made sense to him. Unlike Louise, who was an eternal optimist, Justin had a cynical side that played itself out through lacerating comments that sunk to the heart of matters. Justin made Esther laugh. He encouraged her. But love? No, she hadn't told him that she loved him and he didn't seem to expect it of her. He hadn't uttered the words either. He was still raw from having been left, after 8 years, by his girlfriend. According to Louise, Sheila had moved into town and come out as a lesbian. Her name rarely crossed Justin's lips.

Esther's trail intersected the abandoned logging road

that skirted the property line back down to the front gate. She made a smooth, ninety degree turn, kicking her left ski back at just the right instant. This was the corner where she often fell, sprawling across the powdery snow, the cold sinking into her backside if she didn't get up right away.

From here, a straight-of-way led to the gate and then the driveway covered the last few hundred yards to Justin's house. Her house? No.

Esther's plans to build were burgeoning with the help of Justin's construction manuals. And though he sometimes asked her what she was doing in "all those blank books of yours," this was another secret she guarded. She wasn't sure why, only that it was important to keep some space, some place, as her own.

She sprinted the final stretch to the gate, sliding long and hard, pushing the road back with her poles, all her muscles awake and singing. Her breath came in rhythm with her stride and her thoughts melted away. Step, push, glide. Over and over, she repeated the gestures, like a mantra. Step-push-glide, her heart pounded with dedication and even the twisting in her uterus evaporated with her sweat.

It wasn't until she was past the gate, beyond the Seven Sisters, that she turned to look at them, as if a voice had called out and asked her to stop. And there, in the powdery snow, lay one of the Sisters. Her heavy branches were crumpled and broken among the small pines that squatted in the shadows of the huge trees. Her long trunk was nearly submerged in the snow, except for the ragged end, which protruded fiercely, connected by only a few shreds of wood to the other Sisters.

Esther pushed back the panic that rose to her throat. She felt as if she herself had been ripped up, separated from the clump. She breathed deliberately to calm herself. Why was it, her rational side asked, that she saw herself in the fallen tree and not the ones that remained? And though it helped to be conscious of her paranoia, she could not dispell the feeling of doom completely.

Her skis flung snow out behind her. She pummeled her way to the house and emptied her brain of every last thought as she reached for home.

HELGI ◆ JUNE 1945

SWEET RED JUICE, HELLO. BUT WHY ARE YOU SOUR? IS this really what wine tastes like? Tell me no; I've always thought wine was sweet like honey. But you are good too. I like the way you slip down my throat like a warm mouse and curl up in my belly. What are you dreaming there, mouse?

Oh, says the mouse, I'm dreaming of the hayloft where a little Helgi once hid and listened to the cow in the stable below huff and low quietly.

Oh, says the cow, and I'm dreaming of how the fresh cut hay smelt, made my nostrils flare when you threw some down for me.

And the smoke swallow with the white belly sings to me, I'm dreaming about how you made a hole for

◆ 183

us to fly through, up near the eaves, where the cat couldn't reach.

And Nurr says nothing more than *niau* and pushes his moist nose up into my palm and pleads to be rubbed, so nicely, behind the ears.

I wish I had a tail ... The door opens. Who is it? Just Frau Bogdanis. If I lie still in Sofi's bunk she will think I'm asleep and not bother me. We have more room now that almost half the people are gone from Ingolstadt. Gone, gone, gone. Mamma's friend, Frau Galunas, gone too, to a DP camp. DP, IRO ro-ro-ro-roo.

As soon as we find Isa, as soon as we find an Estonian camp, as soon as soon, we'll go too. And we'll be together. Mamma too. I don't know why they couldn't keep her here. Are there so many more people at the city hospital? Sunday: she will come to see us on Sunday. Our hospital is sending the soldiers home. The Americans are sending the Russians home. The Dutch girl who worked with us has gone home too. Where will we go?

Sofi says she's tired of working for nothing, slave labour, she says. But I don't work anymore, just cough.

The door slams shut with an echo behind Frau Bogdanis. Now where is that bottle? I can't close it anymore — the cork broke when I scraped it out with the knife. Sofi said to watch the things that she got from the American soldiers while she's not here: chocolate, cigarettes, a can of meat with a picture of a striped cat and this wine. I put everything except the bottle under Sofi's pillow.

I pour myself another glass. Maybe I should get in my own bed, up top, so that I won't have to move when Sofi comes. My knees feel rubbery. I hold onto my mattress with one hand and stand on Sofi's bed. The room tilts.

Oh! The wine is spilling. No, no, don't go. I try again. Up pup pup. I swing one leg. No go. I sink down and fall back onto Mamma's bare mattress and empty bed.

It's better to be sitting up. And even better to lie flat.

bayu-bayu, bayu-bayu
muzichok zivjot na krayu

I can hear Mamma's voice in my head, so soft and sweet, singing. I can hear Mamma's voice in my head, whispering but scolding: "Don't sing in Russian Helgi. You know why. Don't." Mamma used to sing it to me a long time ago, when nobody could hear us in our house. But nobody can hear me now. Nobody, nobody.

bayu-bayu, bayu-bayu
odno yablochko upaalo

Yablochko, oun, apfel, apple. The soldier without legs is teaching me how to read German. They have the same letters as Estonian does, and I don't always remember them. Now someone needs to teach me English. I like numbers better — they're the same everywhere.

I count the spaces between the wires of the cot above.

There's no roof to Mamma's bed anymore, the mattress up top is gone and I can see right through the crisscross of springs and wire, like a fence. What's behind the fence? Who's behind the fence? Is it keeping me in or someone out? A bedbug is making his way across the wires. When he gets directly above, he'll jump down on me and bite! Mamma put the legs of our beds in cans of water but the bugs only climb the walls and ceiling and get their dinner that way. The spaces between the wires begin to jump and swim.

Magic bed, where are we going?

Home, Emme's, America? Sofi wants to go to Ammmeeeri-ka and dance. She wants to be a nurse and work in a big white hospital with beds that go up and feed her dog pork roast when she gets home from work. She says that there are no bugs at all in America. Why she's so terrified of them, I don't understand — the bedbugs bite and itch but the cockroaches don't bother us.

All of a sudden the bed moves, sinks in one corner, like someone sitting down on it. My eyes tug open.

IT'S EMME! It's Emme only that she's very white, so white and clear and wavering, like a candle flame. What is she doing here? Emme! I try to call out but my mouth won't make the words. Emme! She doesn't smell sweet and floury like Emme; she doesn't smell at all. I try to sit up but I can't. Her mouth is moving but I can't hear her.

She strokes my leg but I can't feel anything except a low rumble that starts in my head. I squeeze my eyes shut to see her better but when I open them, she's gone. But the rumble has grown and Mamma's bed is turning like a carousel.

Round'n'round around'n'round. I roll out of bed onto the floor and stand up from there, pulling myself up by the bedpost. The metal is cool. Like ice.

But my cheeks are hot, too hot, burning hot, hothothot. The icemetal cools them.

What I need is some air, some of that good bad night air that Mamma always pulls me away from. Some of that cool wicked nice night air to put out the fire in my cheeks. The rumble pulls me toward the windows at the far end and I dance from one bedpost partner to the next, until there is glass against my palms.

Hmmm. A truck in the courtyard. I see. And the light is on outside. There's a truck in the courtyard and it's back doors are gaping, yawning at the black hole where the doors to the hospital basement have been opened. A black square. And the truck rumbles backwards toward it.

Suddenly though, it's quiet. The driver comes to the back of the truck where I can see him. Three other men shrug out of the darkness. One points to the hole. Who lives there? An ogre? Or perhaps an enormous mole that doesn't like any light at all. Have they brought him dinner?

It doesn't seem so. One of the men turns toward the hole, toward me, and I see that it is the deaf man. He's the one who takes the bedpans away and scratches the back of the boy with no arms. When the boy in the bed next to my friend without the legs died, he took him away too. He wasn't sleeping at all.

My chest feels a sudden sharpness. I haven't coughed for many hours, maybe it's time again. But no, only my nostrils flare as I feel a smell rush in, a mushy apple, egg-gone-bad stench, only stronger. Where is it coming from?

You shouldn't turn too quickly, Helgi. You shouldn't turn too quickly, but it's too late because I'm falling already, falling down the wall, down the length of the wall, down the wall, such a long long wall, I slide, and everything slides with me and the walls and the ceiling too.

I hear a bang and a bing, a long pause and then a thud. The floor is cold. I have a hole in my stocking. Mamma will be angry. What are they doing outside? Bang bing pause, thud. I get up — slowly — to see.

The smell slaps my nose again only this time I know what can happen and I hang onto the window sill until the dizziness passes. Outside, the yard is empty except for the truck. I hear the thud and two of the men appear from the back of the truck, the driver and the deaf man. They have hankies tied over their noses and mouths. What for? They jump down and go into the black rectangle of the ogre's den as if they are being dissolved by the blackness: feet first, then knees, stomach and hands, chest and arms and finally, their heads. Drowned.

But then it all happens backwards, first a head, then

shoulders, a stooped back and then hands, carrying something, carrying feet. Those feet come out of the hole first, then legs, a body and another man carrying the other end. There is something wrong with the one they're carrying, he's stiff as a board and there's no stretcher under him. They carry him up the ramp. THUD.

The men jump down empty-handed. After a long time the mute and the driver come back with another man, long and heavy, like a log.

Up the ramp. My stomach flies. Thud. I turn away. Don't fall. In my bed, the thudding continues for hours, maybe years.

There is no rhythm to it but the echo of each thud grabs the bars of my bed and stops the room from spinning a little more. Some women come back from their shifts.

Thud. There is talking, there is quiet and then there is a Thud. When Sofi comes in, all the air moves. She talks to Frau Bogdanis before she comes to our bunk. I pretend to sleep. She looks under her pillow for all her treasures and when she doesn't find the wine, I hear her mutter and look elsewhere. There is a pause and then she talks to me.

"Helgi."

I'm in trouble.

"Wake up you stupid girl. You drank my wine. Didn't I tell you not to touch it. Why don't you ever do anything except lie here?"

I squeeze my eyes shut. Thud.

"I know you can hear me you little rat. Sit up and say something." She grabs my arm and starts to shake me, hissing like an enormous snake. It hurts. Ow. "Open your eyes. That was my wine. I was going to drink it with Peter."

She pinches my arm and shakes me hard. Her hands rain down around my head. I yank the blanket up over me but she doesn't stop.

Thud. "You're just a lazy, stupid, pampered baby. Why don't you grow up and quit pretending? Why? Mamma isn't here to rescue you, what are you going to do now?" Sofi finally stops slapping me but I can feel her get up on the edge of her bed. What now?

She tears my blanket off and looks in my face. I don't dare close my eyes. She says, "I hate you," and throws my cover back over me with disgust.

Underneath, she drinks what's left of the wine from the bottle and mutters to herself until she falls asleep.

The thudding does not stop until late when everyone except me is huffing and dreaming.

How many bodies can a basement hold?

SPRING 1991 ◆

THE THUMPING OF HER HEART FELT SO MOMENTOUS
that Esther wondered that the others couldn't hear it.
The day of her reckoning was at hand. What if the
five people who made up the Seven Sisters collective
accepted her into their fold? They chatted and lounged
as if this day were the same as any other. What were
they disguising? What if they didn't want her? A barely
contained elation and a pungent, creeping dread vied
for her attention. She pressed her fears back into the
small corner of her stomach where she hoped all the
gnawing could be contained.

They were waiting for Gerta. She had run back to
her house to retrieve the agenda for the meeting.
Esther had to think of something, anything, to distract

her from her panic. She lifted her backside out of the deep armchair and rummaged in her pocket for her worry stone. A polished, translucent piece of rose quartz, it was about the size of a large broad bean. She put it in the flat of her palm and rubbed it between her two hands in a circular motion. Louise had given it to her for her twenty-seventh birthday, in the fall. But it wasn't until the Seventh Sister had fallen that winter day that she had taken to carrying it with her, not so much to ward off danger, but her tendency to perceive danger where none existed.

The plunge of the tree had shaken her. The others had thought little of it, joking that perhaps they should change the name of the Land, but nothing else was said. About two weeks after it had fallen, Justin had invited her along to buck up the tree. He had offered her a turn at the chainsaw but she had refused. It would have felt like carnage to dismember an old friend, limb by limb. Instead, she piled the logs into a neat pyramid as Roger snarffled in the snow and chased the snowballs Justin threw for him. She'd learn to use the saw another time, perhaps when she was getting her own wood for winter.

Esther shivered. She looked up from her hands and saw Louise watching her. Her friend smiled encouragingly, comfortably. It would be okay. It would.

"Want me to come sit with you?" she asked softly from across the room.

Esther shrugged and looked back down. Was she

that obviously nervous?

Louise came and sat on the floor at her feet, leaning her back against Esther's legs. Without thinking, Esther began to play with Louise's hair, twisting her dark curls around her fingers. Each ringlet was shot with strands of grey. What if they didn't want someone as young as her? Martin, the youngest member, was five years older than Esther. Would it make a difference? Honour had once joked that it would be good to have some younger members who would take care of the rest of them when they were geriatric cases.

Across the room, Honour sat in one of Justin's straight-backed kitchen chairs, her back support behind her. Honour reminded Esther of Helgi, thin and quiet, yet tender in unseen ways. They had begun a friendship over the winter, over card games of Spite and Malice, 500, and Cribbage; Esther understood that Honour was someone you got to know slowly, if at all.

Martin, on the other hand, was friendly, up front and helpful.

Outside, she heard Gerta scold the dogs — Roger and Samling, Honour's Samoyed — as they cavorted around her. "Down! You damn dogs." Gerta's footsteps clumped up the front stairs. Esther stiffened.

Gerta was Louise's partner. They'd been together for nine years and Esther was amazed at how, in spite of Esther and Louise's friendship, she barely knew Gerta. Though Gerta and Louise lived together, they had separate lives, separate personalities. Esther had never been with any couples who were so good at being together and apart. But what did Gerta think of Esther?

Esther pressed her thumb into the worry stone. Gerta cleared her throat as she sat down at one end of the couch, next to Martin and Justin, who stopped wrangling and turned to face Gerta. Everyone fell silent.

"Well, we might as well start with Esther's application. She's probably been anxious long enough." All eyes turned to Esther and a deep blush rose on her face. It was all she could do to look at these people, these people who were as close as anyone except her family had been. She focused on Honour, whose eyes were obscured behind thick glasses by the reflection of the light from outside.

"Why don't you tell us why you want to join," Louise suggested.

Predictably, Esther's mind went blank. All she could see on the screen of her mind's eye was darkness and a rushing sound. No. She had to say something. Don't wreck it, Esther, don't wreck it.

"This is what I want." Where were the words she had rehearsed? "I mean, I like everyone here and and I feel like you all respect each other and each other's space ..." This was not it at all. Where was her spiel about alternative agriculture? "And ... um ... I like the way you share in the agricultural work and experiment with things ..." Esther's voice trailed off. What did they want of her?

Her heart was thudding hard enough to jump out of her chest. Her throat constricted. This was the feeling she had woken with each night since she had her name put on the agenda two weeks ago. This and a quickly fading memory of a dream, a nightmare. It was as though the demons she had left behind in Winnipeg had struggled out of Alberta snowbanks during the spring thaw and had finally caught up with her. In her nightmares, she was being pursued, chased through houses, away from the Land.

Gerta spoke. "Does anyone have anything they'd like to ask Esther?"

Esther answered their questions about financial contribution, her future plans and other practicalities through a deep fog. Even people's voices were muted and somehow distant. Esther concentrated on her answers and her breath, her fingers moving of their own volition across the worry stone.

From somewhere, a woman's voice — was it Louise? — said, "I want her. Do we have concensus?"

There was no answer.

Esther looked up. They must have nodded because each face sported a wide smile, even Honour's.

"Congratulations!" Louise got up and turned to give Esther a hug. She struggled up from the deep chair. The other four hugged her in turn. Justin held her in a long embrace, her face pressed against his boney chest, and when she unraveled herself from his hug, embarassed with his public display of affection, he leaned down and kissed her. Esther was too overwhelmed to feel anything except relief. She sat back down and brought her worry stone to her cheek. In spite of all the rubbing, it was still cool, and she held it to her burning face. Her heart quieted.

"Why don't we move on to some of the other items on the agenda and give Esther a chance to let things sink in. We'll get back to practicalities later. Okay?"

Esther nodded. The rest of the meeting was a blur. She listened but did not hear. She thought about what needed to be done before she was a full member. Money. What she had saved from working at the lab would be enough for a downpayment, Justin had assured her, and then she could assume paying part of the mortage to cover the rest of her share. She had not even bothered to ask Sofi and Elmar for financial support; they were not happy with her participation in what Sofi called a hair-brained hippie scheme.

But there was something else that she had wanted to ask the collective. Something essential. Why could Esther not think of it? She looked up and scanned Justin's living room for reminders. The pictures on the walls, the books on the end table, the bowl of fruit on the kitchen table and the ropes of garlic hanging from the rafters told her nothing. Her eyes fell on the bookcases that spanned the wall between the living room and kitchen. Her blank books jumped out at her. Yes. Her house. She needed to ask about her house.

Her latest design, the one she had nursed through the long winter, at the desk in the spare room that she had claimed as her own, was five-sided.

Five sides, five senses. Five sides, five directions, according to the Chinese: North, West, South, East and here. Martin, the only one she had shared her plans with, had told her it would be difficult to build, warned her against it.

Five fingers, five toes. It made sense to her. She didn't want anything big, or complex, just one five sided room that would hold her safe. She needed to ask about her house.

Finally, the meeting came back to the topic of Esther's membership and when Gerta asked if there was anything Esther needed to ask, she was ready. "How do I go about picking my building site?"

Justin stifled a startled "what?!" from his spot on the couch and all eyes moved from her to him and back again. What was the problem?

"Don't I get a building site?" she asked, truly puzzled. Louise spoke up.

"Of course you do. Everyone has the right to their own private space on the land," she said and then added, with her characteristic forthrightness, "I think some of us just assumed that you would continue to live with Justin."

Esther glanced at Justin who turned his burning eyes away. What was wrong with wanting her own space? Did he think she wanted to live amongst his furniture, his clutter and his ideas forever?

When Justin finally spoke, there was a familiar snarky edge to his voice. "Well, move over Virginia

Woolf. Women these days need a whole house of their own."

Esther was stunned. But Honour did not let it go. "Chill out Justin. This isn't a blot on your character. Some people just want their own space. You're overreacting."

The room fell into an uncomfortable silence, and Esther wondered if all was lost. She was too numb to feel anything at this point but at least wanted to leave the meeting knowing where she stood with the group. "So am I still in?"

Gerta smiled sympathetically. "Of course. I think we just need to give this issue a little time to settle. Why don't you walk the land and consider where you'd like to build before the next meeting and we'll talk about it then. Is that amenable to everyone?"

"Sure!" echoed from so many mouths at once that Esther wasn't certain that Justin's voice was among them. Yes, she thought, as she closed the door and slipped her worry stone in her pocket, her demons had truly caught up with her.

SOFI ◆ JULY 1945

"I'M GOING TO BREAK MY HEELS PICKING THROUGH this mess."

"Well then, let me carry you!" Peter laughs and turns, his arms cupped to scoop me up, but I back away. I'm too heavy.

"We'll both end up in the rubble, Peter!" Most of the avenues of Munich have been cleared so that cars can weasel their way through. Apart from these lanes, the road is as pebbly and hard to walk as the round stone beaches back home. Blocks of cement, brick and plaster dot the spaces between potholes, some of which are deep and wide enough to swallow a truck.

"I've seen worse," Peter says quietly, kicking at a chunk of plaster, then falling silent.

The darkness has descended since we left the station and the streets are almost empty. It must be close to curfew: nine p.m. The man on the train said that Isa's address wasn't far — maybe a twenty-minute walk.

"Ai! There's something sharp in my shoe." Peter steps closer and I hold onto his shoulder while I empty my shoe.

"Are you sure you don't want me to carry you," he teases and gestures to pick me up again.

"No, I don't. You don't know how heavy I am."

"A little bird like you, heavy? How could that be?"

"Bones. I have strong Estonian bones."

"And mine are strong and Polish. Feel." He holds his arm out for me to touch just as a lame yellow mutt growls at us from the sidewalk. Peter gathers a lump of brick from the street and the dog skulks away with no further warning.

That is when I hear the music. I stop in the middle of the street and cock my head to listen.

"What is it?" Peter asks.

"Don't you hear it?"

"No."

"The music. Mamma says I must have a travelling band in my head, I hear music that no one else can hear. But it's always real, most people just aren't listening for it."

I take Peter by the hand and pull him along toward the next corner.

"You can hear it now, right?" The wail of saxophones and trumpets wafts down a dark, narrow sidestreet.

"Would you care to dance?" he asks, stepping closer to encircle my waist with his arm.

"No, let's go see where it's coming from." I tug at his hand.

He hesitates, leans back so that I can't pull him along. "What about your father? I thought we came to look for him."

"It won't hurt to go see where the music is coming from," I smile, drop his hand and gesture with my head for him to follow me.

He shakes his head doubtfully but comes, lagging a few steps behind. "Sofi, you're crazy. What about the curfew? We'll have to spend the night in jail if they catch us."

"Oh, they won't catch me! I'll just do like I did last time," I cajole. "If it's a party, people will be dressed up. I just want to see." I look down at my own dress, faded and ugly. Maybe now that the war is over, I can find some material and Mamma can help me make a new one.

Peter shakes his head. He's told me he wishes he could buy me things but I know as well as he does that there's nothing to buy even if he had the money. It is quite something that he found me stockings. And he's a gentleman; a man, not a boy with two left feet or groping hands. I've had enough of those.

The music changes half way down the street to "A String of Pearls." I recognize it from the radio. By the time we reach the tall grey house they're playing a tango.

"Let's go in," I plead with Peter.

"But Sofi," he balks "this is someone's house."

"It couldn't be! The music is too loud! Maybe it's a dance place or a big party. Please."

"Sofi, we're not dressed for a party or a dance." I can see that he's grasping at straws.

"Please. It's this or nothing." I open the front door onto a long hallway with a stairway at the far end.

Peter mutters something in Polish, but he follows me down the hall and up the wooden stairs. The music becomes increasingly louder as we mount the dull wooden stairs to the third floor, then the fourth and finally to the garret, where the door stands open. The people inside are talking, laughing, dancing. No one notices us. Peter's hand is sweaty as I take it in mine and step inside.

"No. We're not going in, Sofi," he says, but I let go of his hand and walk in.

Most of the women at the party are dressed stylishly; broad, padded shoulders and hats of all shapes and sizes. A girl leaning against the wall has an enormous peacock feather dripping from her black hat. I have no hat at all.

Peter takes me firmly by the elbow, "Can we go now?"

"Almost. Nobody cares that we're here. Please Peter."

This time he is angry. "NO. Let's go." I spin on my heel. Argh! Everyone. Always, always trying to tell me what to do. Mamma, Isa and now Peter. I take the steps going down two at a time. Damn rules.

"The war is over, you know!" I call over my shoulder at Peter, who is half a flight behind. "Everybody else gets to go to parties. I only get to be young once. Only once and it's almost gone."

I'm so mad I could cry. I'm not going to cry. Soon they're not going to have anyone to boss around. I jump the last three steps down and yank the door open. Peter can go to hell.

The world out on the street is so quiet that I can hear my heart pound. The skin on my back prickles. Where is Peter?

He steps out into the street quietly. Serious. We walk without talking. The street is even more treacherous in the complete dark.

Suddenly, I am in the bottom of a shallow pit.

"Are you hurt?" Peter's voice is at my side.

"It doesn't matter," I say though I can feel a scrape stinging my knee. He reaches in, grasps me under the arms and pulls me out of the hole. It's just then, for some reason, that I realize that I'm going to see Isa. Suddenly, it's real. Isa!

"Hang on." Peter takes hold of my arm.

"What is it?"

"I think this is the street where we turn but I can't see the sign in the dark." We step toward the corner where the air smells strangely blue and acrid. A drunk staggers out of the darkness.

"What ya lookin' for?" he asks with a thick Bavarian drawl.

"Kelterstrasse," Peter answers taking my arm and

pulling me closer to him.

"*Jah, jah,* this is it," he sputters and then, "have you got a cigarette?"

"Sorry," Peter says and we step back into the middle of Kelterstrasse and the drunk is swallowed up by the darkness behind us. The narrow house with our address number and a light in the window appears a few houses from the corner. I bang on the door and stand back to wait. A woman of about forty with smooth blonde hair and a blank face opens it, suspicion in her eyes.

I start in Estonian, "I'm looking for my father. Juhan Leppik. He sent us this address," and, when she doesn't change her expression, I ask, "this is the Estonian camp, isn't it?"

"Jah. It is. But I don't know of any Juhan Leppik." She looks up at Peter behind me as if to ask who he is.

"This is my friend, Peter," I introduce him and he bows slightly and holds out his hand to the woman, says, "pleased to meet you" first in Polish then in German. "And I'm Sofi Leppik."

"Well, I don't know if we can help you, but come in. Come in." She smiles for the first time, a wary smile, and leads us into what looks like a living area. A few women sit at the sides of the grey room and two men playing cards look up.

"This is Sofi Leppik and her friend, Peter, a Pole I think," she says looking our way and I smile. "Sofi is looking for her father, Juhan Leppik. He sent her this address. Does anyone know of him?"

The room mutters a very quiet *tere*, and the bald man at the table rubs his stubbly face.

"Sit down. Please," he commands. Peter sits down next to me. The man plays a few cards, as if he has forgotten us before he turns to me.

"A tall man? You said his name was Juhan."

"Yes. With a thin face." They know him!

"He was here for a week but he had troubles at the IRO office getting his status confirmed, so he left." He turns to the other man, "Remember?"

"Oh, that one. Nice man," the other man answers and lays down a card. "From Virumaa."

"So, he's not here? Where did he go? Do you know? Did he say? When did he leave? Did he say if he was coming back?"

"Please, one question at a time," the man turns and says, scolding me. "He went to Ingolstadt. That was two days ago. He said his family is there. You must've missed him or crossed paths on the way here."

I push back my chair and stand up. We've missed him. Damn damn damn. Where has he gone?

"You can't go anywhere tonight," the first man says without looking up from his game. "It's after curfew. Stay here. There's room."

One of the women comes and takes my arm gently, motions for Peter to sit down again, and leads me out into the hall. She is old and reminds me of Emme.

"I'll give you a blanket each and show you where your room is. You're limping. An injury or did you hurt yourself tonight?"

"Oh, I tripped in the dark. It's nothing." I lean down to look at my knee. A bead of blood has run all they way down to my ankle.

The woman bends to look, "I'll get you something to clean it with." She pats my shoulder gently.

"I'll be alright. It's nothing." And it's true. My disappointment is bigger than everything else. Suddenly I feel tired, so tired that my legs don't want to go up the stairs. I will myself to the top where the woman is waiting, her head cocked to one side, like a puzzled chicken.

"Are you sure you're alright?"

I nod. "I'm just tired. And hungry. And we need a camp to go to. There isn't one for Estonians in Ingolstadt. Is there room for us here?"

"No, I'm afraid not." She wrinkles her brow. She opens a cupboard door and I see that there are exactly two blankets. She pulls them out and puts them in my arms. Two people are away. But they're coming back.

The room has four cots pushed against the two long walls. Two are bare and I throw the blankets over the lumpy stained mattresses. A draft emanates from the window. Why didn't I bring my coat with me? Damn. The bedsprings sag and groan as I sit down. Damn camp. Stupid people. I could scream but then they'd throw us out into the street. I am so tired of this wandering and nobody wanting us. How am I ever going to get to America if we can't even get into a camp?

No point in sitting here. I thump back down the stairs. Peter has joined the card game. I sit beside him as the three men lay the cards on top of one another. Behind me, one of the women starts to hum. The others join in without looking up. Soon the tune finds words and everyone sings. Except me. What is there to sing about, I want to ask them. What?

... *Ah, those eyes, those eyes that I will never forget*
They sing a ballad that we used to sing back home.

... *those beautiful blue eyes on which my heart is set...*
Peter's eyes are blue though he's probably never been a boatman like the fellow the song is about. And though I don't want to sing, when they start with the next one, my voice joins in of its own accord.

A birch grew in our yard
just outside the front door
and was, in my childhood
my dearest, dearest friend
It gave me shade and sheltered me
its sap was fresh and sweet
and the rustle of its tender leaves
cooled my beating breast

We sing one song after another, until it comes time to retire and people nod quietly and disappear to their rooms. Eventually, Peter folds and we go too.

Our room is cold. I yank my shoes off and tuck my feet in under the blanket. Peter's bed howls as he lies down in it. The wool is rough and musty and though I tuck the blanket all around me, I can't get warm. I can't seem to find sleep. I shiver and turn, shiver and turn until I can't bear it any more.

"Peter." I tiptoe to his bed and whisper for him to wake up. "I can't sleep. I'm cold."

He sits up on one elbow and throws his cover half off. He pulls the rough wool blanket from my shoulders and throws it on top of his.

"Come. Sleep here with me. We'll be warmer." I hesitate. What is he asking me? "Don't worry, I won't cause you any trouble. I give my word. Like brother and sister. Climb in."

I curl up close against his chest and he throws his arm around me. For a long time, I can't sleep though I'm finally warm. Peter's even breath wafts across the back of my neck and his heavy arm hugs my waist tighter as he falls asleep. He's a good man. I don't know what Mamma worries about. He would even make a good husband.

SUMMER 1991 ◆

ESTHER PADDED DOWN THE SILVERY DEW-WET PATH in her sawed-off rubber boots. She wasn't usually up this early. The sun had not yet crested the rising hills to the east of Seven Sisters. There was a chill in the mid-summer air. Or was it inside her?

She hadn't slept well. Her dreams were full of houses, some messy and filled with knick-knacks, some too small to find an entrance, others too large to find an exit. The one that had stayed with her, even as she pressed open the howling garden gate, was of a white room whose walls were filled with pictures, postcards and cut-outs from magazines. A man was taking the pictures down while a woman protested. Esther had stood aside, as if invisible, and nodded in agreement with the man. Yes, there was too much noise and happening in the world. It was good to have one white room for peace.

Or a garden. The tomatoes were beginning to ripen, Esther noted as she skirted the tall, staked plants. As she brushed against them, they emited a pungent odour that caught in her throat. Nightshade family, she said to herself automatically and then stopped to look at the word again. Nightshade. What did people — other people — need to shade themselves from in the night? She understood in this moment, how guarded she had become.

Pulling in, little by little. Though she and Justin had talked — but only once — about Esther's desire to build her own place, she knew the issue was not resolved. His resentment leaked out in small ways. She knew he felt abandonned. But it wasn't her who left after eight years. She had promised him nothing. She wished she could tell him this.

Esther surveyed the garden around her. She and Louise had planted almost a half acre, some of it in standard rows and combinations, the rest as experimental plots of heritage seeds, hybrids they had developed themselves and non-traditional combinations.

As she came to her peas, the unsettledness in her chest disolved into a grain of something — dread? sadness? she wasn't quite sure, only that it was hard and pebbly. Her peas. Some so tall that tendrils reached beyond the top of the eight foot wire trellises and strained toward the sky. The flat pods of the remaining snow peas were filling out. Their season was almost over. She'd let a few grow big and others go to seed. But the tall telephones were ready to pick.

Esther parted the dense cascade of foliage and reached for one of the plump, bursting pods. As she pulled it free, the entire trellis shuddered, as if in acute pain, the leaves trembling. She had to say something to him. It had done her no good to remain silent with Sofi all these years. She had to find another way to resist, to claim her space.

She snapped a pod open. Eight perfectly dark green, perfectly compact peas nestled up against each other in a tight, familial row. Why peas, people always asked her. If she held this pod up to them, said "see!", would they understand?

Louise understood. She and Esther were kindred spirits in many ways but their shared curiousity about plants was the key to their friendship.

The gate squealed. Right on the mark. Esther watched Louise, who was wearing only a sarong tucked up above her full breasts, through the foliage. She was sleepy-eyed and intent upon her own inner story. They would not break morning's silence until much later. Louise and Esther could work for hours, pulling up extraneous chickweed, lambs quarters and other so-called weeds, without saying a word.

Esther began to pick in earnest, filling up the basket that hung on one of the trellis posts, and then another. They could shell them during the land meeting that morning, though in all likelihood more would get eaten than tossed into bowls.

Esther's name was toward the bottom of the agenda this time. Martin was facilitating. Everyone sat in their usual places: Honour in the straight-backed kitchen chair, Martin, Gerta and Justin on the couch. Louise sat in the new rocker that Justin had constructed over the winter. Esther's new kitten, still unnamed, batted empty pea pods at their feet.

The meeting had gone smoothly, with some discussion about maintenance work on the waterline. The pressure dropped sometimes, inexplicably. When Martin hiked up to the water box that sat between two large boulders at the side of the creek, it was full of water. Was there silt in the lines? When were the filters last cleaned?

Finally, when most of the peas had been shelled, it was Esther's turn. She cleared her throat and looked at her land partners. It had become progressively easier to speak in their meetings. They were not impatient, did not interrupt, like Sofi, like the people at University.

"I've found a building site," Esther began, with an intake of breath, dropping a handful of peas into the bowl in her lap. "Above the creek, just where the lip of the valley begins to flatten out. There's already a bit of a clearing, some big rocks ..."

Louise and Greta smiled at her widely. Martin shrugged as if to say, why not?

"It might cost you a bit to extend the power to there,

but otherwise, it's a lovely spot." Honour was gracious. She had already told Esther that she would be glad to have her as her closest neighbour. They could make a joint path in the winter down to the driveway.

Esther turned to Justin. His forehead was lined in a deep scowl. Esther's heart dropped into her solar plexus. Uh-oh. His arms were crossed tightly over his narrow chest and even his slouch seemed determined and tense.

"That's one of the spots I go to contemplate life. It has *spiritual* significance for me." He spat out the word spiritual. It was not a concept he used except, Esther thought, when it was to his benefit. The shit. And though she was angry — or was it *because* she was angry? you musn't get angry he has more power than you — she struggled against the fog that threatened to close in around her. Even her own voice sounded muffled when she spoke again.

"So what does this mean? I can't build there?" Esther felt the tears behind her words and resolved not to cry.

He turned to the others, suddenly rational. "Well, what do you think? I know that you all have such spots on the land." He had posed the question in such a way that they could not challenge him without questioning his honesty. And yet, they must know that he was doing this on purpose. How could they not?

Esther slumped into the depths of the armchair, hoping that it would swallow her up. Damn.

Sometimes it was so hard not to feel persecuted, singled out and thwarted. How could she even live with this man now? He had been harbouring this antagonism all along, even as they made love, hiked with Roger, went to pick out her kitten, or concocted a soup together. Esther thought of her tent, which was hunkered down in the corner of her bedroom closet, untouched since last fall when she had taken it down and moved into her lover's house. If she moved out and tried to pitch it somewhere, would every spot become significant to him?

Sofi's voice in her head: *you can't trust anyone except your family.* Over and over. *Can't shouldn't don't.*

The fog closed in. By the time the phone rang and Honour got up to answer it, Esther's senses had narrowed to a thin tunnel.

"It's for you, Esther." Honour held out the phone. "Your sister, I think."

Esther knew before she even grasped the dark receiver that something was terribly wrong in Winnipeg. Kadri would never phone during the day otherwise.

Esther barely heard her sister's breaking voice, "Vanaema died last night."

Silence. But the burning. The grain of dread in her belly had burst and every part of her body went slack as the bitterness seeped into her muscles. Even her vocal chords were not willing to vibrate, to tremble an answer to Kadri.

"You there? Are you okay, Esther?"

"Mmmm."

"Come home right away. We'll help pay for your plane ticket. Come."

Esther hung up the phone and scooped her kitten into her arms. Was this what Sofi had meant? People die when you go away.

The kitten struggled in Esther's hands and jumped down. Louise's arms folded around her. And Esther could not cry. She could not feel anything at all. The fog had closed in completely.

◆ K. LINDA KIVI

MARIA ◆ MAY 1946

BONES LIKE BIRDS. I RIP OUT THE SIDE SEAM OF THE skinny blue dress in one motion. The stitches crackle above the din of women working, scissors snapping, the sewing machines at the far end churning. Very few of the dresses that came in the IRO shipment to our DP camp in Desching fit us but at least now we have real fabric to work with in sewing class. How is it that they grow their women so tall and carrot thin in America?

"Can I borrow the little scissors to take out the sleeve?" I ask my neighbour, whose work table faces mine. She is pinning a checkered wool cloth to one of the newpaper patterns that Madam Lys, our teacher, taught us to make.

"I'll need them again in a little while," she warns me. There are not enough tools to go around and we guard our right to them when we have cloth to work with. The first to arrive in the morning are the first to get them. I was late this morning. Juhan and Sofi were arguing again. The girl wants to go to Munich to a nursing school. Always wanting to go somewhere, wanting something that she can't have. And what does a girl need with so much book learning?

I start picking out the stitches that attach the sleeve to the dress one by one. The Organization people gave us each two dresses in hopes that we could piece something together to wear. Madam Lys peers over my shoulder.

"You could use the sleeve as is," she suggests.

I work out the last few stitches and pull the freed sleeve up my arm and she pins it to the shoulder of my dress. My own dress looks even more faded next to its bright cornflower blue and my red fingers disappear into its length.

"But will it be wide enough for the Frau Doktor?" I wonder aloud about the Doctor's big wife who has arms like piglets.

"Did you measure around her arms?" Madam Lys asks as she grasps the material hanging beneath my arm with her long fingers.

I shake my head, "no, only the length." Madam Lys circles my chair and holds up the other two dresses that will make this one — one dress to buy medicine for Helgi. Madam Lys looks at the dresses with the eye of a professional. She used to own a dress shop in Kiev. She's a lady. This I can see even now that her clothes are almost as old and worn as ours. Even my mule Sofi has had regrets about not coming to the camp sewing school when she saw who the teacher was. But no. There is no way except her way; if she can't go to nursing school, she won't go anywhere. She'll work in the camp creche instead.

What man will want to tangle with such a peppercorn?

"We could cut a strip of grey from this one," the teacher holds up the thin wool dress that is too small for anyone except a child, "and if the blue sleeve is not wide enough, we could sew in a strip of grey on the underside."

I start on the other sleeve, squinting at the threads. My concentration is snapped by the sound of coughing, a terrible rattling cough that makes me shudder. I know without looking toward the office that it's my Helgi. I keep my head down, my eyes on my work, I don't want the others to notice. There has already been talk.

Some women are jealous that Helgi gets to work in the office, learning to keep the books, while they have to sew in this enormous drafty room where the dust of bullet and bomb making is still hard in our nostrils. One woman asked if Helgi and the rest of us wouldn't be better off if she was in the hospital. Another asked if Helgi was already coughing back home. And "has she been tested?" Positive or not, I can take care of her better myself.

But not everybody is whispering and suspicious. Proua Matteson, a woman who knew Kadri in Tallinn, told us of the Doctor. "He has connections in America," she said. Juhan took Helgi to see him. He said he could get us some medicine but if it didn't help, Helgi would have to go to a sanatorium. The closest one is in Munich.

Helgi doesn't want to go. I know. She wouldn't eat at all. The medicine will help. It will.

My neighbour asks for the scissors back. I pull out the last few stitches and toss them with a rattle over to her side.

Helgi coughs again. I get up quietly and go to the office to see her. I pry the door open a crack and have to call three times before she looks up from the numbers she is knitting.

"Mamma," she touches her chest, "what is it?"

"Nothing. I just came to see you. Don't forget to eat your lunch." I pull the door shut and go back to the dress.

One dress and a kilo of bean coffee. The Doctor didn't want cigarettes, so I traded ours for coffee. The Germans need their coffee.

Proua Matteson is at my table when I get back. "Come eat lunch with me," she says and smiles a gapped row of broken teeth. "I have something to tell you."

Over lunch we talk about our class, about the hunt for extra food, about which countries are taking refugees and from which camps. When the other women at our table leave to go back to work, Proua Matteson asks me to stay.

"I know that you are worried about Helgi's lungs," she starts and when I start to protest, she takes hold of my arm. I am surprised by the gesture of warmth from her. Why does she want to help?

She continues, "I got a letter from my sister who is in a camp in Oldenburg, one of the camps UNRRA has taken over. From what she says, their food is better than ours and some of the consulates have started interviewing for immigrants."

I nod and crease my brow. Why is she telling me this after all the other women have gone? What does she know?

"Well, let's get back to work!" her tone changes from secretive back to gay. When we are almost to our tables, she takes my arm again and whispers in my ear, "there is a hospital near Oldenburg too: in Huntlosen. Take her there before she becomes any sicker. She won't be able to immigrate unless she gets better."

I don't need to ask who this hospital is for. But will our other little mule want to come with us? That Sofi thinks that eighteen is old enough to make good decisions. If only she knew that there is no age great enough to make the right decisions in a time like this. Juhan tried to talk to her about the Polish boy but she wouldn't listen. He is a nice man but this is no time to marry, no time to put papers in front of any official who doesn't ask for them.

She won't listen to us anymore, especially since Juhan forbade her to go to Munich. She doesn't understand that we are not safe. Not yet. The Bolsheviks are not far.

The scissors clatter onto my wooden table. My neighbour nods with her chin to where they sprawl, their blades spread wide. My turn. I begin to uproot the stiches of the longest zipper I have ever seen. What else will we find in America?

I pull at the side seams of the grey dress. The thread is good and strong. Juhan says that the American parts for the Jeeps he is learning to fix are all new and strong too. But will America take us? Or Australia? Someone said they ask fewer questions.

There is a murmur in the room. What is it? A man from the IRO office has come in. What does he want? He looks in my direction. He is talking to Madam Lys. Have they found me out? Why are they talking so long?

Madam Lys turns to us. She is not happy. Her lip is curled in a way I have not seen before. She clears her throat.

"They tell me that we are invited out into the courtyard. The men have been invited too." She spits the word invited out in such a strange way that I wonder what has happened. What do they want with us?

"What for?" someone shouts from the far side of the room.

"There is someone here to see us, my friend tells me." She nods to the man and follows him out into the yard. I slip to Helgi's door.

"Helgi. We are all going outside. Something is happening. You stay here." Helgi nods quietly.

I am already out of the door, in the yard, too late to turn around when I see him. I cannot turn around. It's too late. He's come for me. He'll ask to see my papers. He'll see that mine are wrong. No. No.

The red stars on his shoulders are so bright that I cannot look at his face. Russian. I hide among the taller women. The officer speaks to us in German.

"Hm-hmm. I am here in Desching on behalf of my government, the government of the Union of Soviet Socialist Republics, to bring their sincerest greetings to you. I know that many of you come from places that have now joined our honourable struggle against fascism and imperialism. I have come ... "

A young man snatches the officer's cap. He runs. The officer turns, puts his hand on his pistol. His face is beet red. I peek out from behind the women and see Juhan in the back row of the men. The officer turns back to us.

"I have come to invite you back to your homes ..." Such a clamour begins that his words are drowned by the crowd. Someone throws a stick at him but it lands at his feet. He tries to shout over us but nobody wants to listen. After a while, we are quiet again.

"Our peace-loving government knows that many of you fled only because you were afraid of the fighting and had no interest in the politics of the fascist war-mongers …"

People hoot like a flock of seagulls rising up over a stinking fish.

He continues, "… and we will welcome you back with open arms. There are many new collective and state farms in your homelands and in the cities you can participate in the industrial achievements of the Soviet Union."

First they send thousands to Siberia, chase us out of our homes and now they want us to come build their land of dreams in our country. Even the IRO man has to cover his mouth not to laugh out loud. People disperse, muttering. Garbage: they'd do better to stay away.

I am the first back inside. Slowly the other women come back in, chatting and laughing under their breath. One of the last women in, a young Latvian, rushes from table to table whispering something in the other women's ears. Each time, the listeners burst into laughter and the news spreads through the sewing room. Proua Matteson comes to tell my neighbour and me.

"They gave the officer his hat back," she starts, holding her hand in front of her mouth, "and it was — if you'll excuse my language — full of shit!"

I look up and see Helgi in the doorway of the office. I smile at her and put my hand on my heart. It is still pounding hard. Always pounding.

◆ SUMMER 1991

THE BASSO PROFONDO OF THE CHURCH ORGAN reverbated in Esther's bones, pervading the hollowness inside her. The booming, trembling notes were comfortingly familiar as was the musty church air. The old building was cool, even in the August heat. Though she had been coming here, to the old German Lutheran church that Winnipeg's Estonian congregation sometimes borrowed, ever since she could remember, she had never set foot inside during the summer. The whole family, even Bob, when Kadri was still married, had come here every Christmas Eve; Sofi wasn't much for religion but it was one of the few things that Elmar insisted on.

Vanaema had loved this church too. She had believed

in God, not as faith but as fact. Taevaisa, the Skygod, as he was called in Estonian, had helped keep her family safe, all except her husband. Juhan, Esther's grandfather who they never talked about. Before she had gone to B.C., Esther had finally asked Vanaema about him, but Vanaema talked as though he were still alive and Esther decided against asking how he had died. The war, yes, but how? When Vanaema had still been lucid, in the moments between her travels into the past, she had been eager to see him again when she finally went to heaven.

Vanaema in heaven. Esther was glad that her grandmother had believed in such things even if Esther didn't. Elmar had often joked about how the Communists believed that when the old people died, so would the church. Except that there were always more old people to fill the pews of the churches that hadn't been converted into granaries and barns.

Esther peered down the dark polished pew. Helgi, Elmar, Sofi, the boys, and Kadri at the far end. Everyone had the same wooden expression, even the twins, who could not make head nor tail out of the sermon. Neither could Esther for that matter. The minister, an old family friend, filled the spaces between the organ music with a quiet drone of words. Each time, he began with "Dear family and friends of the deceased ..." and though he continued on, Esther couldn't make sense of the words, couldn't hear.

By the time she died, Vanaema had already departed. Sometimes she moved her mouth, Helgi told Esther, but it was as if she hadn't enough air to push the words out. And though she looked into people's eyes, she showed no signs of recognizing even her daughters. "It wasn't long after you left," Helgi said, "that she stopped telling her stories." And it was then that Esther wept for the first time since the news had plucked her from her life at Seven Sisters. She cried, her tears mingling with the sweat on her brow, not so much for Vanaema, but for herself. She cried for the stories that would never be told, for the lost link.

Esther wished that Vanaema had left something else behind besides a closet full of tiny polyester dresses. There was the ruble — yes — and the ladle but ... A diary, letters, a family tree, something that would fill in other blanks, answer the questions that there hadn't been time to ask. But no. Vanaema had never learned to read and write. And though that had always been the way Vanaema was, without question, without thought, Esther suddenly couldn't imagine how anyone could live without the written word.

What had her life been like, really? Before and beyond this time, this land? Later, at the cemetery, the question caught Esther again. The flat grey headstone where the people from church were gathering read "Maria Leppik". But of course. She had a name and a life and fifty years of experience before she ever became Vanaema. Maria Leppik: would it have surprised Vanaema to see the name that others had almost forgotten, there, engraved in stone? Or would she have hoped to see her maiden name?

Even in the burning heat of the sparse tree-cover of the cemetery, a chill shot down Esther's back. What was Vanaema's maiden name? She didn't know. Did anybody?

A serious lump had lodged in Esther's throat by the time she took her place between Elmar and Kadri at the graveside. On the other side of the pit, and all around, were the people of the Estonian community who were their friends and extended family: the greying couples Sofi and Elmar's age, their children, many who had children of their own now, and one lone silver head, the last of Vanaema's friends. As Esther scanned their faces, she was surprised to see the tears in people's eyes. But of course; Vanaema had been a grandmother to many of them too. That, as well as a reminder of who had been missing in their lives. Most of Sofi, Elmar and Helgi's contemporaries had left their gentle, coddling mothers behind in Estonia. And those of Esther's generation had grown up with only vague notions of someone far distant, too far to touch or be touched, who occasionally sent stale, vodka-filled, Soviet chocolates at Christmas.

Esther had had a *real* grandmother, flesh and blood and the loving stroke of the hairbrush through her curls. A person who had left an imprint on her life as surely as the one on the golden ruble. Esther dug into the pocket of the black rayon dress Kadri had lent her and fingered the coin. She had taken it along from Seven Sisters and had kept it with her, moving it from pocket to pocket as she changed her clothes.

Esther stared into the pit where Vanaema's coffin had been lowered. What had Vanaema wanted her to do with the coin? Make home? Hah! What a farce. Just to have someone take it away? If you have to start over and over again, what was the point in starting at all? She knew she was overreacting, but she couldn't seem to stop herself. Why was she so eager to see every possibility of home extinguished. What was she so afraid of?

Esther wiped at the beads of sweat on her upper lip with the back of her hand. Helgi handed her a hankie and when Esther did not reach for it, her aunt placed it in her hand and gave a squeeze of reassurance. Esther flushed hot. What right did she have to be upset? It was Helgi who would miss Vanaema the most. How would she make home without her? They had never been apart.

The minister began to speak again, interrupting Esther's thoughts. Sofi began to weep with deep wrenching sobs as Kadri held her. Sofi's voice in Esther's head again. This time not taunting, just plaintive: *They can't take away what you don't have.* And, *education and health are the most important things.* They can't be taken away. But what about family? What about home, Sofi? You've wanted and had these things too. I know you're trying to protect me, but I want to live too.

Elmar touched her elbow lightly. She caught his eye briefly as he took the twins by the hand. There was water in his eyes, too. His own parents had died in his absence, without even a letter of notification from behind the iron curtain.

Only Helgi seemed beyond tears, somehow stunned or vacant. Orphaned, Esther realized; the word was orphaned.

Esther saw a clod of soil break apart as it fell into the grave. More earth fell on the coffin and Esther wanted to get down on her knees, hike up the hot, black dress and press her hands down onto the earth, like an Arab praying, to send Vanaema safely on her way, wherever it was that she had gone. To heaven or only back to the earth?

Friends came and touched Esther and her family on their shoulders, shook Elmar's hand, patted the boys on their heads even though they were too old for that, murmured comforting words and drifted away to the line of steaming cars. Elmar lead the boys, stiff and burning in their new suits, toward the limousines. Sofi and Kadri followed. Finally, Esther took Helgi's hand and led her away too.

They say that you don't belong to a place until one of yours is in the ground. It made sense, Esther thought as she watched the burger joints and car dealerships whip by beyond the windows of their air conditioned capsule. She felt as though a piece of her own self had been buried. Was this what it would take?

Esther thought of Seven Sisters fondly, for the first time since she left. Maybe it would be okay. She'd find another spot, start building right away so that she'd be far enough along by the time the snow flew. But no, she was dreaming. What did she know about building a house?

The limo pulled into Sofi and Elmar's driveway. The neighbour woman who Sofi had hired to put out the food and wash the dishes, was holding the door open for the guests. Inside, people milled around the laden table, lifting cold cuts of smoked turkey and eel onto their plates, scooping salads.

Elmar took up his post at the improvised bar on the buffet and sent the twins in search of ice cubes from the downstairs freezer. The only Estonian joke Esther had ever heard came to mind: Who's the only one sober at an Estonian funeral? The deceased. Hopefully, people would have restraint. Elmar filled Esther's glass with soda water when she waved the gin bottle away. She stood by the front window and looked out.

She didn't really want to talk to anyone, though there were lots of people there who she hadn't seen in years. Kids she had grown up with but who had all gone their separate ways, slipped into the mainstream of Canadian culture with only their names left to bear witness to their cultural heritage. Did any of them speak Estonian anymore? With anyone other than their parents? Did they miss the roll of rrr's on their tongues? Did they dream that they were being pursued, by men in caps, by bears, like she did?

Esther fielded questions and smiled politely until, eventually, her questioners drifted away. Part of it was that she didn't quite know what to say. She lived somewhere where she didn't even have her own home. And she knew they would look askance at the vaguely communistic set-up of Seven Sisters. What Esther wanted was far beyond their realm of imagining. Perhaps they were right. Perhaps it's best to trust only your own.

She hoped that Justin felt badly about his pig-headedness. She hadn't even looked at him or said goodbye before she met Louise at her car. Esther had felt him watching her. What did he want? What did he expect her to do, to feel? As a member of the land she had a right, didn't she, to her home. Why was it that some people always have to fight for what is theirs, even if that means filling the streets and chanting songs of protest?

Esther slipped into her old room and pulled the door shut behind her. She stretched out on the double bed that had replaced the one that Elmar had built when she graduated from her crib. The room was still except for a thin, incomprehensible muttering that came up through the floor; the television was on downstairs. She closed her eyes. It sounded like the music that opened the news. Must be six o'clock.

A commotion on the stairs, a pounding of footsteps, a confusion of voices, startled Esther from the bed. She rushed into the hall. "What is it?" she took hold of an arm and asked.

Tule. Tule. Come. Said with the gravity that replaces exclamation points in Estonian. A man's voice was calling them down the stairs.

A dozen or more people gathered around the television, their faces already stricken. Esther pulled on Elmar's arm. "What is it?"

"Gorbachev has been overthrown by hardline Communists." There was no need to say more. The Communists would never let Estonia go. She felt the already wilting flower of possibility within her shrivel completely, as if she and that little country she had visited only once, were tied to the same fate. It was all over. A season of hope — Dead.

Esther turned away and felt every last tear suck back into that deep place where a small people survive in spite of it all. No, she could not go back to Seven Sisters now.

HELGI ◆ AUGUST 1947

THERE ARE ONLY THREE ROUNDS LEFT. ANDO AND I only need two more tricks to win this leg. The trump King and something smaller are still in the game. Mustn't lose my lady. Which one of them has the bearded man? If Kalev wasn't distracted, his face would tell me. Eero's is always as blank as a bombed building when he plays Bridge. No help there.

The air is all moving today. I sat down facing the window — not in my usual place — so that I can see Mamma and Isa arrive. The path from the Huntlosen station winds between the trees, where the sand is swirling, a pale yellow cloud beyond the first line of pines. Beyond that are the salty woods that separate the hospital from the Baltic sea. I've only been to the beach once — the seagulls were circling, screaming like air raid sirens over the wide beach. I could only just see the strip of a Friesen Island between the sky and the high waves. I would have liked to go again but Mamma says no.

The sea is in the air today. It has come to me. The salt makes my skin pucker and tingle.

"Helgi!" Ando shakes my arm lightly, "It's your turn. Put a card down."

I put down my low trump — four of hearts. Kalev chuckles and winks at me but his laughter brings on his cough, as it often does. He slaps his King down on the table and turns away from us, toward the wall. He has only one lung left to breathe with — they pricked a hole in the other side of his chest and filled his ribcage with air to collapse his lung and let it rest. The one the doctors left him to use is rotten, too. He clutches his hollow chest as if to keep his ribs in place and pulls for air between the chopping of each cough. Sofi says he's going to die.

Sofi thinks all the boys who were in the mines are going to die. But what does she know? Kalev's temperature is lower on some days and he still gets out of bed almost every day. He even tries to eat what the nuns bring us. She says that everyone knows that sanatoriums are supposed to be in the mountains, that the damp sea air will not help. What does Sofi know. It's only Kalev who coughs so terribly.

When the spasms of his chest calm, I can see from the way he cradles his handkerchief, that it is moist and full. He gets to his feet unsteadily and whispers for us to finish the game without him. His slippers flap down the long hallway of polished brown linoleum, past all the open and closed doors of our wing. We won't finish without him. We never do. He'll be back soon.

Outside, my roommate, a middle-aged Frau, is walking, elbows looped with her daughter's. The daughter comes every Sunday, like Mamma and Isa, though her camp is somewhere else, not in Oldenburg. Sofi comes sometimes but not every week. She says its too far, but I know that she is busy with her boyfriends, as usual. It's only an hour by train from Oldenburg where the Estonian camp is.

"And just what are you dreaming about *tüdruk*?" Ando asks. He calls me "girl" instead of Helgi, to tease me, but I don't mind. Although we sometimes switch, he is usually my partner. They taught me how to play Bismark and Hearts and Twenty-one too, but mostly we play Bridge. You need four for that and except for the old man who doesn't get out of bed anymore, we are the only Estonians at the sanatorium. Eero said it used to be a military hospital, one that they threw together during the war. All the soldiers have been sent home now, just like in Ingolstadt, all except the ones with TB.

"Helgi, hello! It's game time again." Ando shakes the rickety table to get my attention.

He likes to make me blush. It isn't hard. Kalev is coming back, flushed red and stooped.

"I couldn't let our dummy take your hand, he'd lose it to the girl again," Eero says to Kalev. "And she wins too much already." He reaches over and messes up my neat criss-cross of tricks and plays his second last card. Luck has visited Ando and I again — I have the ace of that suit and there are no trumps left except my lady. She scoops the last trick.

"Lost again," Ando crows and bangs the table with his open palm when he sees my queen, "and we won!"

Ando pushes the pot of cigarettes toward me and I hand one of them to Eero whose job is to cut it. He ceremoniously unclasps his penknife, whose handle is the prettiest mother of pearl, and makes the cuts carefully, sure that each piece will be no bigger or smaller than the next. He reaches the first piece across the table to me on the flat of his rough palm, and then hands one each to the other two, keeping one for himself.

We wiggle our cigarette stubs into our cigarette holders. At first, I didn't want my piece, told them to keep it but they insisted it was part of the game. "Besides, Kalev doesn't smoke his either," they had argued. I didn't have a holder. It wouldn't be the same. And I couldn't ask Mamma or Isa for one. So Ando carved me one, almost like his, pale shiny wood with a tiny whiskered troll face in the side.

Ando strikes a match and lights Eero's cigarette and then his own.

"*Tervist!*" Kalev shouts, to health! And I blow the match out. One two three. Ando and Eero lean back in their chairs, balance on two wooden legs and smoke their cigarette stubs, blowing the grey wisps of smoke out into the wind. Kalev and I puff on ours unlit.

I rub the troll's whiskers between my thumb and forefinger. Ando says that soon I'll rub the little man's hairs right off but it's not true. They're only becoming smoother. What do real whiskers feel like? None of the boys have beards; they scrape them off every few days, like Isa except that he leaves his mustache to grow and they don't. Isa's mustache has grown white, like a snow drift on his upper lip.

"What time is it?"

"Impatience, impatience," Ando teases me. "They will come when they come, *tüdruk*."

Kalev looks at his watch and then shows it to me. Almost noon.

My troll smiles. Not so much in his mouth but in his puffy cheeks, he looks ready to laugh at something. What do trolls laugh at?

Ando is good at making things. He carved a twisted pine tree out of a piece of driftwood for Eero's twenty-first birthday. Kalev said it looked like a dead spider with all it's legs sticking up. He's the one who likes to make us laugh. And Eero is the one who knows how to see beautiful things. He almost cried when he unfolded the faded grey layers of the hospital blanket where Ando had buried his present.

Ando carved it all in secret, probably during the rest periods. I don't mind lying there, quiet and still, but I know that Ando gets restless, wants to go walking or work with his hands. The nuns scold him a lot. "How will you ever get well?" they ask and pull at their habits, annoyed.

Maybe Ando doesn't want to get well yet. There was one boy who Sister Brigitte caught putting his thermometer in his hot tea so that they wouldn't send him away.

Sofi says that she's going to Canada. They're taking men to work in logging camps and mines and women to go to families or hospitals. She says they'll pay for the passage but each person has to work for a year to pay it back. Sofi put her name in for an interview right away.

"Is it time for magic marbles?" Kalev breaks the silence of our thoughts.

I smile at him. He already knows that I'll say yes because I like those funny rocks of his. He brought them from the mine in Belgium, where the boys worked while they were POWs. That was before they came to the sanatorium. The English took over the camp and sent the sick ones away.

Kalev fishes the rocks out of his baggy trouser pocket and jiggles them in his hand. He turns the rocks down on the table and takes his hand away. The rocks are odd shaped and, every time, they come up in different patterns. We pretend that they are valleys and mountains, plains, and so on. The first person says what country they resemble.

"Sweden," I start. The other two groan. They're tired of this game. "Stockholm," Eero says, so that the cities are done. Each person has to name something about that country, not repeating any one kind of thing, until we can't think of any more. Kalev usually wins.

"Fiords," Ando adds. "They're not Swedish," Kalev protests. "The fiords are in Norway."

"How about another hand of Bridge?" It's obvious that Ando doesn't want to play. He hates losing. So the cards come around again. The nuns and doctors walk up and down the hallway but they don't bother us. Kalev doesn't have another fit. This time I am the dummy so that I can watch for Mamma and Isa. Ando and I win again. The others groan and Eero cuts the cigarette. Ando lights the match, Kalev shouts *tervist*, and I blow out the match.

Two puff smoke. Two puff air. I watch the wind tear cones from the trees. It is fierce today, as though the sky were coughing as hard as some of us. My morning temperature was barely above normal today and my bed clothes were not soaked with sweat when I woke up. When I'm better, Mamma, Isa and I will be able to catch up with Sofi in Canada. Mamma and Isa want her to wait for us, but she's twenty now. She says nobody can tell her what to do anymore.

Eero's hand is on my shoulder. "What? Is it Mamma?" I look toward the path but there's no one there. Eero lifts my chin up with the tips of his fingers and points toward the top of pines. On the tallest one sits an enormous bird, so big that I can see its curved beak. It flaps its wings to keep its balance on the swaying summit of the tree. What is it waiting for, looking for?

"An eagle?" I ask, quietly, as though my voice could scare it away.

"No. A hawk." Eero answers. I look back down. No Mamma and Isa yet. I look back up. The hawk twists her head around, watching the world as though she owns it. And with a drop and a sharp flap of her wings, she catches the wind and sails toward the sea. What will she do there? Catch some fish perhaps?

Still no Mamma. "She'll come," Eero assures me, as though he knows what I'm thinking.

"But," Kalev asks, with a twinkling eye, "will that crazy sister of hers come too? You'd like that, eh Ando?"

Ando? My sister? What? He fiddles with his penknife. "Keep your ideas to yourself," he says, not looking at me. Eero starts to whistle. Kalev starts to cough, quietly. Ando sulks.

"Sofi is going to Canada." The boys all look up at me, their eyes suddenly big. "The consulate is interviewing for workers. Then she has to take a medical test."

"Well," Ando starts, "that's another place we aren't going."

"No." What are they saying? "We'll get better. We'll go too. You'll see. All of us." They say nothing, try not to show me what they think, but I see it. They think that there is nowhere for them to go. But no. "Who will I play Bridge with if you don't come along?"

And then, I think of something that I hadn't thought of before.

"Who blew out the match before I came?" I ask. It is as if the wind swirled in the hinged window and carried everyone's breath away. The boys are all quiet. They look at one another.

"August," Ando finally answers quietly.

"August Savipea," Eero says.

"August Eduard Savipea," Kalev adds, "the man with three names," and they all laugh uneasily.

"He was a Saaremaa chap — from the islands." Eero looks away quickly, out the window. "Your mother, Helgi! Look, it's your mother coming up the path, isn't it?"

Her head is bent down against the wind and she clutches her kerchief at her throat to keep it from blowing away. She looks like a boiled potato in her faded brown dress and as small as ever. Mamma! I thrust my troll at Ando. He keeps it for me when Mamma and Isa visit because I don't want them to think that I smoke cigarettes. Where is Isa?

I hurry down the long, brown hallway, stretching my legs as long and far as they will go. The wooden door opens just as I get there. Mamma reaches up and pats my cheek and smiles.

Armas laps, dorogaya, she repeats, first in Estonian, then without thinking, in Russian, "dear child, dear child." She pulls me close.

Kus on Isa? "Where is Isa?"

"Sick."

Sick? "Him too?"

Him too.

◆ FALL 1991

SIGH. A BLANK. ESTHER HAD BEEN STARING AT THE
letter she had yet to write for so long that the page's
blue lines had begun to sway, the date at the top like
a lone bird above the waves. It would be nice to be
able to fly. Just pick up and flap away.

Three weeks had passed since Vanaema's funeral and
what had turned out to be a failed coup. Yeltsin had
rallied the Russian troops and the people, in support
of Gorbachev. The hard-line had been defeated. Yet,
Esther hadn't been able to shake the aimless vibration
that wandered through her bones. Mostly, she moped
around Helgi's house, opening and closing the half
empty kitchen cupboards, looking for something that
she couldn't name. No amount of stale Ryecrisps and

plum jam quenched her aimlessness. Each night she fell into a dead, dreamless sleep and woke up to more of the same. It wasn't that she didn't have answers, it was more that she didn't quite know what the question was.

Helgi moved in and around her house, went to work and came home, with a groundlessness similar to Esther's. They ate dinner in companionable silence then taught each other card games, playing them over and over until they fell into their respective beds. Esther couldn't imagine having to get up and go to work but Helgi did so without complaint. She even thanked Esther for cooking dinner every night, as though she didn't expect anything of her niece at all. Perhaps, Esther thought, she should just stay and pick up where Vanaema and Helgi left off. Sofi wouldn't like that though.

Esther had been avoiding her mother. She worried that something more would be expected of her, the daughter, now that Sofi's mother was gone. No, Esther had enough of her own expectations, enough of her own guilt.

Brenda had come to visit, twice, to haul Esther out into the world. "You're depressed," she said. "You won't figure anything out sitting here."

They had gone to the university, done the round of Esther's former colleagues, her prof, who had tried, once again, to convince Esther to come back to school. He probably thought she was wasting her talent on the soil and worm reality of farming. How did someone study agriculture and have such disregard for those who were actually doing it, she wondered? No, it was too late to go back. She had crossed sides.

And when their wanderings hadn't cheered Esther, Brenda had concluded, "You need to go home. Get on with things."

The problem was that she was no longer convinced that home existed for her. It was as if her options were not between one place and another but between being somewhere and being nowhere at all. Her limbs felt heavy, so weighty that she could barely lift them in the mornings. The coup had done it. Her third strike. She was out of the game. It didn't matter that Estonia had emerged from the frenzy of mid-August with a declaration of independence that had yet to be stamped out. Nor that Boris Yeltsin had rescued the Russians by drawing the people out into the streets, like a bear swiping a hive — bees, honey and all — out from a rotted trunk. That was them. This was her.

What to write to Louise? She picked up the pen again and carefully inscribed "Dear Louise" under the date. There. But what now? She couldn't just say "I can't", though these were the words that raced through her veins, like the chant of angry protesters in her ears. Esther had to do something.

She put down the pen and massaged her hands. Even after three weeks of relative inactivity, they were still rough and calloused. And they seemed to be the only part of her body that still possessed some will. Esther had turned Helgi's compost one day and mowed the tiny lawn another. Vanaema's garden, though, was so overgrown that Esther let it be. Rich soil likes the company of roots. No, Esther's hands definitely wanted something more than the flaccid days they spent hanging at her sides. They wanted a steering wheel, a hoe, an axe, even Justin's throat. Something.

What now? Who were Estonians if they weren't opposed to the Soviets? What had she ever been taught about living for something instead of against it? What exactly was she for?

A longing to part the cedar boughs and slip into the dark woods beyond the garden back at Seven Sisters overtook Esther. She was for climbing a ridge, scrambling down a mossy slope, squatting on the hard, cool bulk of her favourite boulder by the creek and watching the water slip past. She was for being left alone to live peacefully. But once you're alone, then what? To fill up strife is obvious, but how does one fill up peace?

She took the pen in hand without thinking, looked down at the page to see that she had written, "I miss the trees." And my grandmother, Esther thought. Yes. The house seemed so house-like, just a plain structure of wood and stucco and appliances, with Vanaema gone. Esther had tried to convince herself that there was no point in mourning. Vanaema was old, she was tired, she was already gone, in her mind at least. It had been the right time for her to die.

But mourning wasn't about the dead. She knew that,

too. Esther pushed back the kitchen chair and stood in the doorway of Vanaema's room. Sofi and Kadri had emptied it of most of her things, sending her clothes to the Sally Ann and dividing up her costume jewellery and knick-knacks among the family. There had been no bickering over who got what. Vanaema never had anything of monetary value, never wanted presents that cost more than a few dollars. It was as though she had been afraid to put pieces of herself into things.

Things can be stolen, broken, crushed. Having invites the evil eye. It is important to hide the things you value, even if they are your dreams. Did anyone know that Vanaema had kept the ruble in her shoe all these years?

Esther felt a phantom hand slide across her hair and looked up to see the small liver-spotted hand in front of her again, squeezed tightly shut. Helgi was the only one who knew that Esther had the ruble. "Keep it," she had said when they sat across the kitchen table from each other the day after the funeral. Helgi had examined the golden coin, turning it over and over in her hands as if she would eventually discover a new side, one that would tell her something the coin could not. Finally, she handed it back to Esther, saying, "she gave it to you for a reason. Keep it."

Oh, Esther would miss Vanaema. She already missed her quiet way of comforting, no questions asked. If she went back to B.C. she'd miss Helgi too. How would she manage alone?

What was it like for her to live in this little house she had shared with her mother for most of her life and never hear the soft padding of Vanaema's footsteps in the halls. Helgi said that sometimes ghost odours woke her in the night and she'd go to the kitchen to see if she'd left something on the stove. But no, never.

Footsteps thunked on the front stairs and the mail slot squeaked open. The non-descript hand of a letter carrier pushed a wad of letters through. Then the Estonian newspaper that came once weekly from Toronto fell to the floor. Esther gathered the mail and carried the paper back to the kitchen. The cards of condolences continued to arrive, a few every day, in their square and predictable envelopes. There was also a long envelope and Esther turned it over to see her name on it.

"That's me," she said aloud. It was from Louise.

◆ K. LINDA KIVI

SOFI ◆ SEPTEMBER 1947

THE SHIP HEAVES AND SIGHS, ALL ITS METAL creaking as it pitches into yet another trench between the swells. The ocean has been rough, nothing but rough, since we left Cuxhaven. And since we got out onto the open Atlantic it's only been worse. Pitching, rolling, one sick-making motion after another. People have disappeared to their bunks in the holds, their clothes stained yellow from the food that they couldn't keep down.

My food seems to stay in place. We can eat as much as we want. Imagine. I tried to get work in the kitchen but everybody else wanted to be there too. They put me here, in the dispensary. People are so sea sick they can barely come for help, their faces green and their eyelids heavy and half closed. They come clutching their bellies.

Almost all of the Ukranians have been sick. They come the most often. Then the Poles and White Russians, the Lithuanians. Estonians and Latvians seem to have the strongest stomachs — I must have inherited mine from Isa.

Isa. He didn't want me to go. But what am I supposed to do in a country that's been shredded by war? Nobody wants to stay. He was so angry with me when I told him. Mamma was quiet but I knew what she was thinking behind those fierce eyes of hers.

"Wait for us! Wait for us!"

"And how long will that be?" I have never shouted at him before. But enough of my life has been wasted. Enough.

There are over a thousand people in this transport. We are among the first, among the lucky. Even the sick ones know it. Those who aren't sick yet stay inside and play cards. The dining room floor is littered with stray fours and jacks, looking like children who have lost their parents. Playing cards, playing cards ...

I'd rather sit in the dispensary, thank you. Soon, I'll be sitting in a real hospital, with real patients instead of just soldiers and people who haven't got enough to eat. With my first pay from the hospital in Winnipeg, I'm going to buy a whole pork roast, a vat of sauerkraut, a crate of white bread, a basket of potatoes, a bag of oranges, and eat it all myself.

Isa says I'm selfish. Mamma says I don't have any

feelings at all. What do they expect? I have my own
life. Canada isn't going to take Helgi. I told them that.
"She's sick! She's got TB! They don't want sick people!
They only want healthy people who can work, *kurat!*
Like me!" Like me. Isa's face turned grey, like his hair.
Maybe I shouldn't have said it.

There are three of us from the Estonian section of
the Oldenburg camp in this transport and then a few
Latvians from across the road. Mostly, people are going
to Toronto. Only one other — the quiet boy with the
limp — is going to Winnipeg with me.

Toronto is near a lake, someone said. And a big river
flows through Winnipeg. Apparently it's flat there,
full of wheat fields like the Ukraine. Someone else
said that's where the cowboys and Indians are. I saw a
film in Bremen with the man they call Jann Vain. He
looked alright, but who wants a cowboy? I want a
husband who washes behind his ears.

The last time I saw Peter was at the station when we
left Ingolstadt. He gave me his picture and asked me
to remember him. I was glad he didn't ask me to stay.

Isa got me the address of some Estonians in
Winnipeg, people who've been there since the last war.
The man has a construction company. Isa is afraid I'll
get into trouble without someone older looking over
my shoulder. I've managed so far. I have managed. At
least they don't know differently.

I never told them about the times when there was a
close call, the Ami MPs who drove me home in
Ingolstadt, and that other time, the soldier had already

ripped my dress … Kadri saved me that time, hit him on the head with the bloody sheet she was carrying, yelled at him in German until he let me go. I never went into the basement of the hospital in Tallinn again. Kept my eye on those soldiers. Some of them were so sweet, so nice. I told her right there and then, after I stopped crying, that if I ever have a daughter, I'd name her after her. Yes, that's what I'll do.

I wonder where Kadri is now? Whether she'll come to Canada too, or go elsewhere? And Birute and Felix. And Peter. Tiiu, Kaja, Alma, Sulev and Jaak?

How do you find anybody in a country so big? They say it takes four days by train to get from Halifax, where we dock, to Winnipeg. It must be as far as Siberia. Hopefully not as cold.

"Sofi, hello." Ursula trips into the room as the ship lurches sharply. I grab her by the arm to keep her from falling. These damn door ledges are a hazard to stockings and shins.

"Saved you. Have you come to relieve me from boredom?"

"Changing of the guard. Have you had any patients today?"

"Just Herr Blum. He said his liver could not deal with the food. Too rich, he said. He was in one of those camps. He looks healthy though, don't you think?"

"I think he likes you, Sofi."

"Oh, don't be silly. What would a Jewish boy do with me?"

"The same as a gentile boy, silly." Ursula picks up the record of treatment. "What did you give him?"

"What do you think I gave him, a kiss on the cheek!"

Ursula doesn't laugh, changes the subject. "Have you been sick yet?"

"Not yet, and hopefully never." I grasp both of my thumbs. "Me neither." Ursula looks at my hands. "What are you doing?

"Holding my thumbs. For luck. Don't you do that in Lithuania?"

"No. Maybe that's what keeps you all from being seasick." Ursula laughs.

"Here. Sit down." I pat the hard polished chair. "It'll be over soon." I pull on a lock of her hair and turn to go. "I'm a free woman now." I step over the ledge back into the hallway. "See you later."

The clicking of my heels on the metal floor echoes in the passageway. My shoulders hurt. Damn this crappy brassiere. I move one strap over and massage the welt that it's left. My period must be due because they're digging in even more than usual. They better have good brassieres in Canada.

"Oh! Salme! You startled me." We nearly bump into each other as we turn the same corner, in the same hurry.

"Where are you rushing to? I was just coming to look for you." She pushes her limp blonde hair away from her face.

"I was coming to look for you."

"What is it?"

"Nothing." The lines on her face relax and she smiles wanly. "You're done working, aren't you?" she asks.

"Ya. Which way today? Toward the old or the new world?" We joke that if we walk toward the front of the boat, it might get us to Canada faster, but once you are as far forward as you could go, there's only one direction left: back.

I fall in behind Salme who walks quickly, like she usually does, toward the front of the ship. The ship pitches and rolls in the swells and we hang onto the walls of the narrow corridors as we go. The *Samaria* is a troop ship, one of the few that survived the war, and they've put her into service ferrying us to the new world. The New World. What does a new world look like? What does a new world feel like? Do people look each other in the eye?

No one wanted to stay in Germany. No one, Isa, no one at all. Not even some of the Germans. People are going wherever they'll be taken in. America wanted families, Canada and Australia, mostly singles. Healthy people. Young people. People who can work. Like me.

But they haven't gotten who they expected. The ship comes up under my feet suddenly, and then falls away again. It is all I can do to keep from pitching head first. Salme pauses to hang on too.

Almost everyone lied at their interview. Anything to get in. Everyone knows the stories. Doktor Orav told them that he is a farmer's boy, and that he has only five years of school. He pretended to stumble over some of the words when they gave him the newspaper to read aloud, but it got him where he needed to go. Canada wanted labourers, not educated people.

And I am going where I need to go too. Do you hear me, Isa!? I am going where I need to go!

Why couldn't he see that? Salme told me about a man who took the newspaper from the interviewer and started reading like a professor. The interviewer didn't understand Hungarian so it was all the same to him what the man was reading. He could have gotten away with it, if he hadn't been holding the paper upside down.

What's going to happen with Mamma, when she sits down with that paper? She never learned to read the Roman alphabet, not Estonian, not German. And she can't ask for a Russian paper.

I couldn't wait for them. I just couldn't. What if they don't pass the tests? What if Mamma doesn't pretend to read right? What if Helgi's lungs never get better?

Mamma turned her back on me when I said that. I was only telling the truth. But they didn't want to hear it. They didn't want to hear anything.

I stop in my tracks. I said, "Helgi is going to die. Just like those boys from the Belgian mine." I shouldn't have said that. I was so mad. It was too late.

Isa even raised his arm. He's never hit me before. Never. "Sofi!" Salme shouts from further up the corridor. "What's wrong? Are you sick?" She walks back toward me.

"No. No. I was ... I was thinking about my father."

"They'll come to Canada soon, too."

"We had an argument before I left. It was terrible." Salme says nothing. Both her parents are on board. All of them are going to Toronto. Together.

"Come on." Salme takes my hand. Just around the corner is our usual spot. This is where Salme comes to smoke. Her parents don't know that she does. They wouldn't like it. Sometimes I take a puff of her cigarette.

"Can I have one of my own today? I'll pay you back."

"Sure. You don't need to pay me back. There'll be lots of cigarettes in Toronto. Lots."

Lots of everything. How will we know what to choose? There will be everything that we can buy. Everything and anything.

"Who interviewed you?" Salme asks as she takes a long drag at her cigarette. "The tall one or the bald one?"

"My luck was running low that day. I got the bald one. I heard the other one was good looking."

"He was," she smiles quietly to herself. He was a Canadian man. Tall and thin with a straight nose and brownish green eyes. The one that finally accepted my papers was tall too. Maybe there's more room to grow in Canada.

I take a small drag at my cigarette. I don't pull it into my lungs. I'll just cough. I lean back against the oblong metal door that leads somewhere we've been told not to go.

The ship rolls and Salme leans back with one foot against the wall behind her. She is very leggy and has small high breasts. Nothing like me. But my hair is thicker, and wavy, even though it's not blonde. Some of the boys think she's uppity.

"Toronto," she says, expelling a sheet of grey smoke. "It sounds so bold." She looks down the hall. "It's too bad I have to cook someone else's food, clean some big house and take care of a horde of children for a year."

Salme is going to be a housekeeper. Her mother too. They think they are too good to be scrubbing floors. Salme's mother used to teach literature at the university. Her father is an engineer.

"What's your father going to do?" I ask.

"The railroad." Isa used to work on the railroad back home. Isa, I'm sorry. He and Mamma came to see me off in Cuxhaven but we didn't have anything to say to each other. Mamma kissed my cheek. Isa held me hard against his chest. We didn't cry. We didn't cry.

The tears come now. I turn my face away from Salme and pull on my cigarette. I don't stop them. They roll down my face and splatter on the grey floor.

I'm sorry, Isa. I am. But I had to go. The New World is waiting.

FALL 1991 ◆

ESTHER PUT HER PALM AGAINST THE COLD OVAL window. Clouds clustered below, a thick layer of down between the airplane and the earth. The plane must be over Alberta by now. She wished the white batting would part so that she could see the mountains rearing up from the foothills, marking her passage across the distance.

Seven Sisters awaited. Esther had to go. She did. After the letter from Louise had arrived, with all its news of the land and everyone there, Esther had known she needed to move, to act, to do something, whatever that something was, to break the hold the events of August still had on her. But knowing she needed to go and wanting to go were two separate things. It wasn't until Esther had read the letter again, carefully, that the news about her kitten had caught her eye.

Esther's kitten, the one who had defied naming, was lost somewhere in the woods. Esther imagined it mewing, plaintively, at the edge of the forest with no place to go. How long could it survive a forest full of owls and ravenous coyotes? Now that she was on the plane, pitching headlong towards the mountains, her desire to rescue the cat intensified. She needed to go look for it. Maybe it would be long eaten but at least she would have looked. At least that.

She put her hand to her solar plexus. The barely submerged fury that lay there turned, like a baby growing in her womb. She pressed it down again, as she had been doing for the the past few days, burying it beneath smiles and words of goodbye. But she did not try to extinguish the flame in her belly. It kept alive her determination to deal with her situation at Seven Sisters, whatever form that would take. Even going back was something.

Esther rooted in her fanny pack among her money and papers for the tube of Rolaids. The chalky tablet broke into pieces between her teeth as she crunched down. Brenda said she was proud of Esther for going back. She was the only one Esther had told about the events at Seven Sisters.

Fortunately, Esther's family had been too absorbed in Vanaema's funeral and their own grief to ask her about her life. Oddly, it was Sofi who seemed the hardest hit by her mother's death, not Helgi, and in spite of Sofi's tendency toward melodrama, her anguish seemed truly genuine. What was even more puzzling was Sofi's attitude toward Esther. Esther realized, after a while, that Sofi was avoiding her too. When Esther caught her mother's gaze, she would turn away as though Esther was responsible for some terrible, unnamed deed. But what? Was she angry that Esther was leaving again?

Kadri had driven her to the airport. Louise would pick her up. Esther spotted a gap in the clouds and caught sight of the quartered sections that were expanses of gold, yellow and burnt umber. Grain. Soon there would be rock. Mountains. How much snow would have fallen in the high valleys? Winter would be at hand in only a few months, the seasons flipping from dry yellow to wet white overnight. At least that was what happened the year before.

On the phone, Louise had assured her there was still time enough to build.

"Martin says he's set aside all of October to help you. He's got all the tools you'll need. Honour's back won't stand hammering but she says she'll keep the crew watered and fed."

"The crew?" Esther had been stunned by this barrage of generosity.

Louise continued, "Gerta is already scrounging for materials — windows, doors, wood and whatnot. Between the five of us, you'll have a cabin by the time the snow flies."

"And Justin?" The question had slipped out before Esther could contain it.

"I'm afraid you'll have to resolve things with him yourself." The words were hard, even in Louise's gentle voice.

"But the spot ..."

"You'll have to pick another one. He's unlikely to run interference again. He knows we're not happy with his antics. We all want you here — happy."

Another spot. How simple. Louise's unquenchable enthusiasm and optimism never ceased to amaze Esther. What did it take to believe that good things would unfold in one's life? Was it something you could learn?

Just before she left, Esther had asked Helgi to tell her the story of the pots and pans again, about how she and Vanaema had buried them under the pine that was no longer there.

The story had a different feel this time. Was it because Vanaema was gone or had something else changed? The sad tale, veined as always with Helgi's muted sorrow, concealed something else. Vanaema had believed they were coming back. Otherwise they would not have hidden the pots. To her, in spite of having been exiled already, it was not a forgone conclusion that once pushed off their land, it would be forever so. In spite of the marching armies that had trampled the rich earth three times over — the Soviets occupying and then withdrawing, the Nazis pushing in — they had not crushed hope with their booted heels.

Why had Esther's family failed to pass that feeling on to Esther?

Why were they all at a loss now that Estonia had thrown off the shackle?

The Estonian community had become a dazed contingent of somnambulists, particularly those of Sofi and Elmar's generation, going through the motions of their daily lives.

The reality of Estonian independence had shocked them all. But why? Shouldn't they rejoice? So let Estonia be free.

Great. Wonderful. She was Canadian. Yes. Finally, she had been freed from her duty to uphold the banner of the free Estonian. Her term had expired. The people in the old country could do it themselves now.

Yes. Free. Then why did her stomach hurt? Why was she still terrified, even more than ever before. If she failed to make a place for herself at Seven Sisters, there would be no excuses to fall back on, no cultural destiny to accuse, no room to stand the eternal victim's ground.

Esther shifted in the narrow airplane seat as if to shoulder a burden more comfortably. Yes, she could hunt for the kitten, build a house with the help of friends, make peace with Justin, but there was more to it than that. Would she ever be able to dispell the notion, buried deep in her gut, that home was not a place that could be counted on? This was the question.

The stewardess' voice announced their descent.

Esther pulled her seatbelt tight and stared into the enveloping clouds. It wasn't until they were almost ready to land that the earth jumped back into view. She hunted for Louise's truck in the parking lot of the small airport but could not find it.

When she stepped into the terminal, she saw why: Justin was there to meet her instead. Esther could not hide her disappointment quickly enough. She saw the corners of her ex-lover's thin lips fall, as if he had understood, only in that moment, that their relationship was over.

They drove back to the land in silence. The things that Esther had to say knotted in her belly and would not unravel.

MARIA & HELGI ◆ JANUARY 1948

KALLIS SOFI,

Mamma and I have some bad news. Isa is dead. It came upon us so suddenly that we haven't known what to do with ourselves. The funeral was three days ago. People from the Oldenburg camp organized it. You know who better than we do.

It was terrible, Sofi. He had been drinking with his friends, you know the concoctions they make and the things they put in it. They brought him to the barracks unconscious. You've seen for yourself how he has come home that way. Mamma put him to bed. His skin was yellow and when I touched his forehead, it was cold. He murmured in his sleep. The next morning he began to cry out and moan. Mamma sent me to get the doctor.

He took Isa to the clinic right away. Mamma stayed with him for three days but wouldn't let me see him. And now he's dead.

Isa's friend, the one who plays the violin, sold Isa's wedding band and had a coffin made. It was just a plain wooden box and there wasn't enough money to buy a stone for the head. The man who carves from the next barrack made a wooden cross but it's plain, Isa's name isn't even on it. Mamma wants to know if you can send money to buy Isa a stone? Our interview with the immigration people is in two weeks. If they let us go, we should come in the spring. Can you send the money before that?

We are going to ask to come to Winnipeg so that we can be together. There are only the three of us now. Can you tell us more about Canada? Mamma wants to know what kind of cooking pot it was that threw your peas up onto the ceiling. She is worried that they won't have the kind she used at home.

Mamma wants to know about your boyfriend. You said he's Estonian. What is he going to do when he's finished working in the woods? Does he have a name, Sofi? Is he tall?

Mamma and I still don't have any suitcases. Mamma is afraid to go to the Russian consulate like the others do to get piles of propaganda papers and have them pressed into cardboard. I've been collecting scraps that I find here and there but it takes so many. At this rate, I'm not sure when we'll get suitcases.

Mamma says that we have written enough. Our hearts ache. We came so far, and now for this to happen.

Mamma prays that you won't be too sad. Isa would have wanted for us to build new lives. We think of you and of him every day. Please think of us too.

Mamma and Helgi

P.S. I am writing this part after Mamma put the letter in the envelope. She didn't lick it yet. Mamma didn't cry at the funeral but I know she is very sad. She hasn't wanted to eat and I heard her sobbing quietly in the night. It feels like a bad dream to me. I wish you were here. You always know what to do better than I do. What if Mamma dies too?

P.P.S. Three days have passed and the letter is still not pasted shut. The man who took pictures at the funeral gave us three. Mamma said to send you one. See how our breath hangs in the air. It was so cold. Someone in camp knows a man who will make a headstone for twenty American dollars. How much do they pay you at the hospital? If I go to work in someone's house, will I get paid too?

P.P.P.S. A letter from Kadri came from England a month ago but this envelope will be too heavy if I put it in. A woman from our camp went to England. She met Kadri and gave her our address. She is working with a family. She says it is terrible and that she would like to go else- where. She writes that the English treat them like white slaves. Here is the address; you can write to her yourself.

◆ LATE FALL 1991

ESTHER PATTED THE LARCH LOG THAT WAS INSCRIBED with the squiggly lines of worms' work. She followed the odd patterns that scratched their way across the surface of the wood with her finger; it was like notation for modern jazz. Pity to burn it, she thought as she slid the heavy metal cover of her woodstove to one side. Sparks flew as the log fell into the blaze. She added a piece of birch and closed the lid just as the bark caught fire, crackling like gun shots.

She brought her hands to her face and inhaled the ripe odour of pine sap and wood smoke. The smell reminded her of her time in Estonia, where almost everyone still heated with wood, still cooked on wood stoves.

Some of Esther's friends from Toronto had returned to the "old country", their laptops and degrees in hand, to help reconstruct, make Free Enterprise out of the ruins of a state controlled economy, set right the life of a confused nation. Would they lose their singsong North American accents? Would they stay?

Were they willing to give up their worst fears? Were they willing to give up the refuge of exile, of being the wronged ones?

Were they willing to live in possibility? Did they know that tears must be wept even after the source of sorrow has dried up?

Did they understand that anger must be raged even after The Villain has fled?

Did they see that villains can wear many faces, take many forms? And that home is never a given?

Esther surveyed her house. The walls weren't finished yet — the pink fuzz of the insulation still exposed — but the essentials of shelter, an insulated roof, floor and walls, doors and windows, were all in place. Running water would have to wait until next year. She could bath at Louise and Gerta's and haul water for cooking and drinking from Honour's.

The pale blue wooden chair Esther pulled close to the stove was one of a pair Gerta had rescued from the dump. It creaked under her weight; she'd reglue the joints when she refinished it sometime in the winter. Her land partners had also scared up a makeshift bed, a card table, a slab of plywood for a kitchen counter and some planks for shelves. All she'd bought was the woodstove. It amazed her how she could be happy with so little. Sofi would be horrified but she'd fix it up by the time she and Elmar came to visit. If they came to visit.

Home. The simple act of building had made it that in a way she'd not expected. But did she know anything more about home than when she began to wonder?

Perhaps not intellectually. But something had shifted in her heart. It wasn't that her occasional nightmares had abandonned her completely, or that she never feared. It was more that now there was a context for belonging. A form.

Home, Esther decided, was not a point, a place, or a spot. Home is the way in which points join. It is a grid for reference only, not a firm, fixed thing that never alters. Home can grow. And shrink.

Home is where you are. And sometimes it's where you aren't. Home is the trick of going on. And the trick of going on, Esther thought, is nothing more complex than simply going on. Nothing had been resolved between her and Justin and yet they managed to co-exist on the land with only occasional friction. In the weeks and months that followed Esther's return, Justin kept his distance. He did show up now and again at her building site to watch the others work but it was as if he were looking for evidence to support his wounded ego. And little by little, Esther ceased to care. They were equals; he had no power over her. It was important to believe at least that.

Esther was not eager for the inevitable day when they would air their grievances, though it had to be done, if not for herself then for her land partners. It was not fair to tear asunder the place that had taken her in. The tension between Esther and Justin wore at them all. What the next round would bring was hard to say. Some grievances are never resolved.

Esther pulled on her rubber boots and retrieved the golden ruble from the secret pocket in her jacket. It was cool and unaccountably heavy in her palm. There was one last thing she wanted to do before the ground froze solid and the snow came.

The shovel leaned against the outside wall near the door. She grasped its cool wooden handle and stepped down onto the bare earth. Even the arrival of November, with its dry wilting plants and grey sparseness, had failed to depress Esther this year. The months of hard work, hammering the frame of her house together, screwing down the metal roof, fitting windows and doors, the gathering of her wood for the winter and the daily tasks of hauling water, eating, just living, had solidified Esther's body with something less perceptible than muscles.

Esther wandered around the small clearing that surrounded her house, stopping to look at the ground here and there. She needed to find a place between the tree roots. She chose a spot to one side of the clearing, below the large kitchen window.

The shovel bit into the earth. The ground was already hard and dry. She put the small scoop of soil next to the the hole and plunged again. On the third dig, a dark flash of fur flitted past the corner of her eye.

It was only Nurr, the kitten who had defied a name, and evaded Esther's search through the forest until she found her one chilly morning, curled in her sleeping bag. The cat had pushed her wet nose into Esther's neck, wanting in, wanting the warmth of the thick down around her. She had begun to purr, scrawny and ratty as she was, as though she had spent no time in the wilderness at all. It was the kitten's purr, a soft Estonian nurr, that had finally pointed out a name.

Nurr curled herself around Esther's calves, niauing. She scooped the cat into her arms, pushed her face into the ruff of fur at Nurr's neck and whispered to it in Estonian. When Esther had told Helgi about the kitten finding her and how she had come upon the name, Helgi had fallen quiet on the other end of the telephone line.

"What is it?"

"Nurr was the name of the cat that we left behind in Estonia."

Esther hadn't known. Vanaema had never told her. There was a lot that Esther didn't know. A few weeks after Esther had returned to Seven Sisters, Sofi had called, hysterical, weeping without respite over the telephone, saying, "See. It's true. People die when you go away," over and over again.

"Vanaema was old," Esther had answered, a little puzzled. "It was her time to die."

"But Isa wasn't," Sofi had answered, sending a shock down Esther's spine. Elmar? What had happened to her father?

But before she had time to ask, Sofi continued, "he was only forty-six. Only forty-six. If I hadn't left, he'd still be alive."

Elmar was sixty-three. Who was Sofi talking about? *Kes Mamma*? "Who, Mother?" Esther had asked. "Elmar's not dead. Is he?"

"Not Elmar. My father. Juhan. Isa." And with this she began to weep again, squeezing out forty years of sorrow. And guilt? Why was her father's death her fault? How did he die then?

"What happened? Tell me."

"We fought. He didn't want me to come to Canada without the rest of the family. I wanted to have my life. I was so tired of the war. I was young, I didn't know better."

"But how did he die?"

"I shouted at him when he forbade me to go. I shouted at my own father, my protector, my dear father."

"Mom. Shouting at someone doesn't kill them. How did he die?"

Esther held the phone away from her ear as Sofi wept with renewed fervour. Esther was stunned. She had never heard Sofi fall apart like this. Like a baby, with abandon. Had she been holding this in all these years. Guilt.

"It's okay, Mamma. Cry. It's okay." Sofi had told

Esther the story of her father's death when her sobs
quieted. How Juhan had survived the war only to kill
himself by drinking contaminated liquor. Esther
wished she had known her grandfather, had asked
Vanaema more about him.

Nurr struggled in Esther's arms, wanting down.
Esther took the shovel in hand and began to dig again.
Would Sofi ever believe that she wasn't at fault? Perhaps not, but at least the secret was out. The boil was
lanced.

The hole was about a foot deep and a foot wide.
Esther dug in her pocket for the ruble and laid it in
the bottom of the small pit. No. What would happen
to it if she put it in the ground like that, bare gold
against bare soil? Would it tarnish? Decompose? Wear
away until there was nothing left but a thin sliver of
shine? And did she care?

No. And yes. It needed something more. Some company. Esther peeled a strip of bark off a small birch at
the edge of the clearing. It was so thin it was almost
translucent, a pale glowing whitish-pink.

She wrapped the coin in the paperbark, white side
out, and laid the package into the hole, luminous
white against the black soil. Now all she needed was
something blue. She dug in her pocket for her hankie
of blue cotton. She tore a corner off and laid it in the
hole. There: blue, black and white. The colours of
Estonia.

She pushed the earth into the hole with the side of
her boot and got on her knees to pat the soft mound

smooth. She would dig again in the spring, not here, but over by the house, just a small salad garden and flowers. Esther didn't know much about flowers. Somehow, in the translations of place and culture, Sofi, Elmar, Helgi and even Vanaema had never acclimated to the flowers of the new world. Apart from the clumps of daisies that Elmar grew and Vanaema's irises, Esther knew little about things that blossomed for the sheer beauty of it.

Honour would help her pick seeds from the catalogues they got, thick bundles of colour to pore over during winter storms and long nights.

She would plant irises to remember Vanaema by.

A patch of daisies for Elmar.

And some bachelor's buttons — the Estonian national flower — for home.

◆ ◆

Acknowledgements:

For those who shared your stories — Arnold and Niina Kivi, Ivi Valgre, Ando Kallas (in memoriam), Peter Baltgailis — thank you, thank you. For comments, encouragement and direction along the way, I am grateful to Ginger Mason, Patricia Warkentin, Nicola Harwood, Irene Mock and Ann Alma. A special thanks to Brenda Brooks for editing and Michelle Benjamin for seeing me through the morass of publishing. Lastly, thank you to Joanne Hetherington, Karen Warkentin, Tika, Aya and all my other friends for their persistent support and love.

Thank you to the Explorations program of the Canada Council.

The Polestar First Fiction series celebrates the first-published book of fiction — short stories or a novel — from a Canadian writer. Polestar is committed to supporting new writers, and contributing to Canada's dynamic and diverse cultural fabric.

Polestar Book Publishers takes pride in creating books that enrich our understanding and enjoyment of the world, and in introducing discriminating readers to exciting new writers. Whether in prose or poetry, these independent voices illuminate our history, stretch our imaginations, engage our sympathies and evoke the universal through narrations of everyday life.

For a copy of our complete catalogue, featuring poetry, fiction, fiction for young readers, sports books and provocative non-fiction, please contact us at:

POLESTAR BOOK PUBLISHERS
1011 Commercial Drive, Second Floor
Vancouver, British Columbia
CANADA   V5L 3X1
(604) 251-9718